D1531806

Weaving Destiny

G.P. Ching

Carpe Luna Publishing

Books by G.P. Ching

The Soulkeepers Series

The Soulkeepers, Book 1
Weaving Destiny, Book 2
Return to Eden, Book 3
Soul Catcher, Book 4
Lost Eden, Book 5
The Last Soulkeeper, Book 6

Other Books by G.P. Ching

Grounded

For Aaron, Madi, and Hannah

Contents

Glossary of Terms

Healer (pr. n.) A rare type of Soulkeeper who has the power to heal people and situations. Healers can tell right from wrong even in the most confusing of circumstances.

Helper (pr. n.) A type of Soulkeeper specialized in the art of equipping Horsemen for their work.

Horseman (pr. n.) A type of Soulkeeper who acts as a warrior, battling Watchers when all other tactics have failed.

influence (v.) Act of placing a human under the spell of a Watcher. Usually, Watchers will lure their victims to drink an addictive elixir that subjects the person to the Watcher's will.

red stone (n.)An enchanted gem given to another Soulkeeper by a Healer that allows the Soulkeeper a window into the Healer's abilities. It is given when the Horseman or Helper needs guidance over an extended period of time away from the Healer.

Soulkeeper (pr. n.) A person with a recessive genetic abnormality that gives them power to fight Watchers. Each Soulkeeper's gift is as unique and individual as a fingerprint but their purpose falls into three categories: Helper, Horseman, or Healer. A Soulkeeper's power is triggered by a stressful event and is only fully realized when the person accepts their true purpose.

soulkeeper's staff (n.) A branch of the tree that grew out of Oswald Silva's buried corpse. Used by a Soulkeeper, the staff acts as a portal, transporting the user from one place to another. Makes a sound like a firecracker when activated. Also known as an *enchanted staff.*

Watcher (**pr. n.**) Angels who defected with Lucifer from God's grace. Also called fallen angels or demons, these beings have the skin and eyes of a snake, and wings like a bat. They are skilled in illusion and sorcery, appearing as model-perfect human beings most of the time. They are notoriously lazy, preferring to wait until their victims are physically or emotionally weak to attack. They live below ground in a place called Nod because the sun drains their powers. They gain strength by eating human flesh obtained by abducting people and keeping them as slaves.

Chapter 1
Closer

Katrina Laudner ached to be noticed. Within the crowd of college students in the living room of Sigma Nu fraternity, she danced, careful not to spill the contents of her red plastic cup. Her denim skirt scarcely hit her upper thigh. Her cami scooped dangerously low. And the thump-thump of the music the DJ blasted from the corner pounded its way out of her body in a rhythm of invitation. No one noticed. Even half naked, she was wholly invisible.

"What are you drinking?" a velvet voice asked. He was close, close enough for her to hear over the deafening music, close enough to feel breath on her earlobe. Katrina stopped dancing and turned. A boy stood between her and the wall.

1

"The red juice from the back," she answered.

He was exceptional in his stillness. The strobe light made the rhythmic mass of people to their left and right jerk with the illusion of disconnected movements. But like an inanimate object, the light had no effect on his image. Every flash was the same.

"Are you here alone?" he asked.

"Yeah. I was supposed to meet my roommate but she never showed."

"You're not alone anymore." He stepped in closer. Navy blue eyes, almost purple, set off his pale skin and black hair. The overly confident smile on his lips did as much to entice her as did the hard line of the jaw it was attached to.

She took another sip from the red cup. The juice she'd scored from the man in the back was spiked with something that burned her throat on the way down. She hoped it made her nice and numb. Maybe then she could play it smooth. Guys could smell desperate a mile away.

"Do you know there's alcohol in that?" he asked.

"Are you a cop?"

He laughed, a dark, hollow sound that caressed her ear like a lover's kiss. "No."

"Then I can safely say that if I didn't know it was spiked before, I sure as hell know now. I'm pretty sure this stuff could remove nail polish." She drank again, but couldn't stop herself from peeking over the top of the cup. Wide shoulders, pierced eyebrow—he was rock-star, chiseled-by-the-gods gorgeous.

He wrapped his hand around her upper arm and pulled her forward, bringing his lips to her ear again. "It's just … you look underage," he said.

"I'm old enough." The heat from the spot where his skin touched hers was almost too much to bear. She went back to dancing a little, breaking the connection.

"Hmm. A lawbreaker, I think. What should I call such a reckless and wild one?"

"Katrina."

"Do you have a last name or am I to assume you're so infamous that you don't need one?"

She tilted her head to the side and smiled. "Laudner. Katrina Laudner. What's yours?"

"Cord."

"Cord like what you open the drapes with?" she teased.

"No." His expression darkened. "Cord like what you strangle someone with."

Katrina took a small step backward. She thought about leaving altogether but then his face relaxed into a teasing smile. He was trying to be funny.

She shrugged off a foreboding weight that had settled on her chest. That was the problem with growing up in Paris, Illinois. She wasn't used to anyone different. She was too cautious. "Do you have a last name, Cord?"

"No," he said. The corner of his mouth tugged upward as he looked over the bump and grind on the dance floor. "Infamous."

"Nice. I'm beginning to think it begins with a B and ends with astard."

The smile melted from Cord's face, replaced with an intensity she'd never seen before—well, maybe in some wild animal show where the predator was about to eat the prey.

Katrina crossed her arms over her chest as if the position could deflect the raw power he'd turned in her direction. An intoxicating scent drifted over her, cinnamon, sandalwood, a dark forest. Closing her eyes, she breathed deeply through her nose. She was about to compliment him on his cologne when Cord's touch made her eyes flip open.

He'd moved in closer. While her eyes were closed, he'd stepped forward until the back of his hand brushed the bare skin above her elbow. The contact made her ache to close what little space was left between them. It stirred something deep within her. Every inch of her became super sensitive, her flesh reaching out for him, knowing he was the source of some unknown thrill.

A hot blush crept across her cheeks. She distracted herself by lifting her cup to her lips again, but it was empty. Had she drank it all so quickly?

"Can I get you a refill?" he asked.

"Yeah."

He lifted the cup from her grip, never breaking eye contact. "I'll be back in a moment. Don't move, Katrina Laudner."

She didn't. He slid gracefully between the gyrating students toward the back, giving her a delightful view of the taper of his hair down his neck, wide shoulders, and dark jeans that hugged the curve of his hips. She wasn't going anywhere. In fact, if he asked her to stand there all night, she might comply.

A new song thumped from the speakers and the crowd went nuts, throbbing to the industrial rhythm. She joined in, arms reaching toward the ceiling.

"I like this music. What's it called?" Cord was beside her again.

Startled, she stopped dancing. "Oh my God, you scared me. Shit, you were fast."

Cord handed her the red cup, full now. "Do you know this music?" he asked.

"I think it's from the nineties. Um, 'Closer' I think. Yeah, it's called 'Closer.'"

"I like it."

She sipped her drink, aware that his purple eyes scanned every inch of her as if he were trying to see under her skin. Unnerved, she shifted away from him.

"Hey is this the same punch? It tastes different ... like cinnamon or something." Katrina took another sip and felt the burn travel all the way to her toes.

Cord shrugged. "Where are you from, Katrina?"

The room began to sway and she reached out a hand to steady herself against the wall. "Paris, I'm from Paris, Illinois."

"Paris?"

"Yeah, I know. Don't blink or you'll miss it."

"Oh, I like small towns. I've been meaning to visit Paris."

"Really? Why?" A foggy weightlessness caused her to lurch forward.

"Are you okay?" he asked.

"I think I've had enough. I better quit while I'm still sober enough to find my way home."

"That sounds ultimately responsible. Was I wrong about your reckless and wild ways?"

She laughed. "I have my moments."

In front of her, his muscles shifted beneath the drape of his shirt. It was some kind of silky cotton, not too tight, not too loose. The gray fabric beckoned her to reach out and run her hand up his abs and across his chest. Thanks to the red cup, inhibition had packed its bags. On impulse, she rested her palm on his stomach. She swayed on her feet.

A hand caught her lower back. Cord pulled her into his body, effectively holding her up. Taller, he had to lower his chin to meet her eyes.

"You smell good," was all she could manage. The room floated away. He was her tether to the Earth.

"May I walk you home, Katrina Laudner?"

There was no hesitation on her part. She wanted to fall into him, to press every part of herself up against his hard body. She wanted to cover herself in that delicious smell. "Sure, that would be nice."

He reached for the now empty cup in her hand—when had she finished it?—and nested it inside his own before setting it on the floor near his feet. Something about the action bothered Katrina and she found herself staring at the cup. A headache bloomed at her temple.

"Are you going to leave that there? I mean, I could find a garbage can. It's rude." Her voice sounded muffled, like she was hearing herself through a thick wall of glass.

"Don't worry about it. It's okay just where it is."

Katrina was normally obsessive about neatness. It bothered her that he wouldn't pick up after himself. But at the moment, she had more pressing issues. "Whoa," she said, weaving toward the door. "Whatever was in that drink went straight to my head."

Cord half carried her through the crowd. Once they were out the door, the fresh air revived her. A moment of clarity came halfway across the deserted walkway of the quad.

"What was in that drink?" She shook her head and inhaled the crisp night air, stepping away from Cord, whose cologne suddenly seemed overpowering. Disoriented, she stumbled toward the gnarled trunk of an oak tree, planting her hand on the rough bark.

"Stay close to me, Katrina," Cord said. "Girls shouldn't walk alone. You never know who or what could be lurking in the shadows."

Much clearer now, Katrina blinked her eyes and focused on Cord. In the lamplight, the black hair and purple eyes, so sensual at the party, looked menacing. The shadow of the tree she leaned against seemed to reach for him, like his presence was a magnet to the darkness. The silhouettes bowed and stretched, rippling under the illumination of the lamppost. Shadows weren't supposed to bend that way. The air wasn't supposed to ripple.

"I think I'm hallucinating," she said from the harbor of the tree's branches. "I think there was something other than alcohol in that drink."

She closed her eyes and shook her head again. Had he drugged her? She'd heard of boys slipping things into girls' drinks. Every college girl had. She was so stupid. What was she thinking, leaving the party with a stranger?

"Relax," Cord said. His arm snaked behind her shoulders.

When had he moved so close to her? He'd closed the gap between the walkway and the tree in what seemed like the blink of an eye.

"Wait. I need to get home, Cord. I'm not feeling well."

"Lie down right here, Katrina." He lowered her slumping body to the grass.

Part of her wanted him. He smelled good. He felt good. But a larger part of her knew something was wrong. She'd been drugged, that was for sure. The hard, cold ground cut unevenly into her back.

"Wait," she said, her voice barely a whisper. "Let's go back to my dorm."

With his arm still behind her shoulders, he leaned over her, his face hovering with the promise of a kiss. "No, Katrina," he said. His purple gaze cut the darkness. "I want to talk to you. I want to know all about you. I want to be closer."

From behind heavy lids, she tried to respond, but she was transfixed by the curve of his lips. She closed her eyes and tipped her chin, an invitation for him to finish what he started.

Nothing.

When she opened her eyes again, Cord was gone. She was lying next to the tree, the glow from the lamppost illuminating an empty walkway at her feet. She sat up, wondering if she'd hallucinated him all together. Man, what was in that drink?

On autopilot, she stood and walked back to her dorm. Her brain felt fuzzy. Exhausted, she let herself into her room and stumbled through the darkness toward her bed.

"Ohmygod, Katrina. I've been so worried about you!" Mallory said. Katrina heard a click and the soft glow of her roommate's lamp made her blink. "First, I couldn't find you at the party and then you weren't here when I came home. Where the hell have you been?"

"What time is it?"

"Four in the morning."

"Four? Really? Shit, I don't know, Mallory. I think someone slipped something into my drink. I feel weird."

"Into your drink? What, like a roofie? Are you okay? Do you need me to walk you to health services?"

Katrina thought about it for a minute. "No. I feel okay. I don't think anything happened. I just need to sleep it off."

"Well, the good news is it's officially spring break, so you can sleep as long as you want."

"Yeah, spring break. I'm supposed to go home to Paris tomorrow ... I mean today, later. Hell, I've gotta get some sleep."

Katrina didn't bother to undress. She slipped beneath the covers of her bed and closed her eyes. She was asleep before Mallory turned off the light.

Chapter 2
Work to Do

Malini Gupta was not the sort of girl who gave up easily. When she said she was going to do something, she did it. Despite being half past four on the Friday night of spring break, she concentrated on the task before her. She sliced through shiny pink foil with determined precision, ignoring the growing pain in her middle back. The floral knife Mr. Laudner had given her to use scraped across the stainless steel worktable. She handed the shiny square to Jacob, who folded the foil around a pot of blooming tulips.

"How many more of these do we have to do?" She rubbed the place where her shoulder met her neck.

The backroom of Laudner's Flowers and Gifts was packed with dozens of spring plants in shipping crates. "Looks like maybe a hundred," Jacob said.

"Damn, really?" Malini whined.

Jacob shook his head. "Don't complain to me, Malini. You're the one who wanted this job. I told you it sucked."

"I need the spending money. Plus, it was an excuse to see you." She'd been grounded from Jacob since last fall when they'd lied to her parents about taking an impromptu road trip. The honest truth was much worse. They'd been in Nod, where Malini and Abigail had rescued Jacob and his mother, Lillian, from the Watchers, the fallen angels who wanted their souls. But, of course, telling her parents that her boyfriend was a Soulkeeper, a warrior who protected human souls, was out of the question. So, they'd lied. Now, her father was convinced Jacob was a bad influence.

Without her job at Laudner's Flowers and Gifts, she would rarely have a chance to see Jacob now that school was out. Sure, they sometimes used the staffs that Gideon had enchanted from the branches of Oswald Silva to visit each other at night, but they always had to be careful not to get caught. Lately, it seemed like their entire relationship was a series of stolen moments.

"I know it's hard right now, Malini, but it won't be like this forever. Your parents will come around. Have you asked them about prom yet?"

"Prom? Jacob, I can't even get my dad to agree to let us study together. I hardly think I've worked up to the junior prom. Besides, it isn't even until May. We've got like a month and a half."

Jacob reached over and ran his hand down the line of her wrist, linking his fingers with hers. "I can't wait."

At his subtle tug, she leaned in over the tulips, her lips reaching for his, needing the reassurance of just one kiss. He pulled their linked fingers to his chest. For a precious moment, the only thing in the world was his face, the warmth of his breath, and the brush of his lips.

"What's going on in here?" Lillian Lau called from the door to the backroom.

Malini withdrew to her spot opposite Jacob. She smoothed her shirt and tightened her ponytail.

"Nothing, Mom," Jacob said.

"Well, do less of nothing and more of foiling those pots. I just sold another ten to the Westcotts. Fran says she's lining her porch with them. Her older daughter, Stephanie, is coming home on spring break and adores tulips. Isn't her son, Phillip, in your class?"

"Uhm ... yeah," Jacob said.

"I thought so," Lillian replied.

Malini caught the look Jacob shot her and kept her mouth shut about Phillip. He'd been part of a group of kids who'd made their lives hell last year along with Dane Michaels. Dane had come around when Jacob rescued him after he'd gotten his ass kicked by a Watcher. They were friends now. But Phillip didn't like it. In fact, the new friendship with

Dane had given Phillip one more reason to hate Jacob and Malini.

Lillian looked at her watch. "You guys are on the clock for one more hour. Stop messing around and get the rest of those done. I don't want to have to explain to John that you didn't get your work done because you were fooling around in the backroom. He'd have you on separate shifts in a heartbeat."

Jacob sighed.

"The answer is, 'Yes, Mom,'" Lillian said.

"Yes, Mom." Jacob turned his back on his mother and widened his eyes at Malini. The corner of his mouth pulled downward into a lopsided grimace.

Malini pressed her lips together and cut another foil square to keep herself from laughing. The telephone rang. Lillian retreated to her place behind the counter to answer it.

"Saved by the bell," Malini murmured in Jacob's direction. "There's always someone watching."

"It will get better. One way or another."

"What is that supposed to mean—"

Lillian was back in the doorway. "That was Abigail. There's been a killing … a homeless man in Chicago. She thinks it's Watcher activity. They're forming a team to investigate and bringing in another Horseman from the area. She wants us there tonight so she can fill us in on the details. I told her we'd come directly at the end of our shift."

"But I can't," Malini said. "I'm still grounded. I've got to go straight home."

"I'll talk to your father, Malini," Lillian said. "I'll explain you need to stay late."

"You mean you'll lie for me again. What if we get caught? One more slip up and my father could lock me up and throw away the key."

Lillian glanced at Jacob, who folded his arms across his chest, jaw clenched. "That's a chance we'll all have to take. It's the price of being a Soulkeeper," she said.

Malini slammed her knife down on the workbench and shot them both a dirty look.

"Excuse me," she said. "I need to use the restroom." She walked quickly, afraid the sting in her eye would turn into something more. The door closed behind her.

"Malini," she heard Jacob call. She pretended she couldn't hear him.

"Was it something I said?" Lillian asked.

"Mom, could you be a little more sensitive. She's not…"

Jacob didn't have to finish. Everyone knew exactly what he meant. She wasn't a Soulkeeper. After months of meeting with Dr. Silva, of mysterious herbal concoctions, physical tests, and more talking than she'd cared to do, nobody knew what she was. The worst part was, no one would admit what she suspected all along: she was nothing. She wasn't a Soulkeeper. No matter how often they included her or how many tests they did, it wouldn't change the truth. She was nothing more than an ordinary human girl with an overdeveloped sense of smell that just so happened to allow her to detect fallen angels.

* * * * *

Malini, Lillian, and Jacob arrived at Dr. Silva's gothic Victorian in Jacob's dilapidated blue pickup truck. Once they were far enough into the thick of the maple orchard, the budding trees provided enough cover to camouflage the vehicle. Each of them had told a story about where they were supposed to be that afternoon. Each of them lied.

"Just in time." Dr. Silva held the sunroom door open for them. Her pale eyes were as disturbing as ever but the jeans and pink Henley she wore were a far cry from the head-to-toe black she insisted on wearing before she met Jacob. "Gideon and I are going to open the portal. We need to do it in the tower where there's more space and less chance of prying eyes. Come." She tossed her platinum hair over her shoulder and led the way through the kitchen.

Malini followed, down the hall, and up the stairs to the library. A tapestry of the four horsemen of the apocalypse hung on the wall. She balked when she saw Dr. Silva charge through it.

Jacob took her hand. "Close your eyes and jump. Trust me," he whispered into her ear. "The wall's an illusion."

Reluctantly, she followed his instructions, opening her eyes in a small room on the other side. The floor was wood. A spiral staircase made of wrought iron twisted up the center.

"Where are we?" she asked.

"In the tower," Jacob replied, tugging on Malini's hand to usher her up the spiral after Lillian.

"In all the time I've been working with Dr. Silva, she's never brought me here," Malini said.

"I'm sure she has her reasons."

"Just like you're sure she has her reasons for blowing off our training sessions or wasting my time chatting for hours about nothing."

Jacob shrugged.

At the top of the stairs was a large room with a sanded wood floor and windows that stretched to the ceiling like a lighthouse. A desk and bookcase lined the inner wall where the tower was connected to the house and a telescope stood next to the windows. Gideon waited in the center of the cleared space in his angel form, his wings folded against his body. His aura cast the room in a bluish-white glow.

"Hello, Jacob, Lillian, Malini," he said, nodding his head of wild auburn hair in their direction. His green eyes lingered on Malini, who was embarrassed to be caught staring. It was hard to look away from Gideon when he wasn't in his usual form as Dr. Silva's red cat.

"Nice to see you again, Gideon," she said, breaking the awkward silence.

"Shall we get started?" Dr. Silva grabbed two wooden staffs that leaned up against the wall by the desk. She handed one to Gideon. "If everyone would stand back, we'll bring in our other team member."

Malini took a step toward the windows. Dr. Silva and Gideon faced each other, tapped the staffs together, and then pulled them apart. Their muscles strained with the effort.

Between the two staffs, thin blue fibers stretched like electric taffy. A girl formed within the blue web. She stepped out, looking around the room as if she'd landed on another planet. Gideon and Dr. Silva closed the portal behind her.

To Malini, the new Horseman was the one who looked alien. She guessed the girl was not much older than herself. She wore a hooded leather jacket over a clingy, gray sleeveless T-shirt and skinny jeans. Her lips were too red, the lower one pierced with a metal stud. A hot pink streak of hair fell from her widow's peak to her chin. As the girl turned to face Gideon, Malini noticed a tattoo on her neck under her jet-black ponytail, but from where she stood she couldn't make out the details. Everything about her was hard, tough, unarguably a Horseman.

But she also had a figure. She reminded Malini of one of those girls in a video game, all muscles and boobs. If that wasn't enough to make Malini feel inadequate, the girl's roving peeps landed on Jacob. Her eyes worked their way from his head to his feet, then back up again. When she reached his face, she stood up straighter.

Malini tucked a strand of hair behind her ear and hugged her stomach. Maybe, after this, she could start working out.

"This is our new Horseman, Mara Kane. She comes from Chicago. She witnessed the kill."

Mara did not attempt to shake anyone's hand. Instead she reached inside her jacket and pulled out a sucker, the cheap kind they gave away free at the bank. She yanked the wrapper off the red candy top and popped it in her mouth. She rolled it across her tongue as she turned toward Dr. Silva. "When do we start?"

"It's nice to meet you, Mara," Lillian said with exaggerated zeal. She extended her hand to the girl, who shook it without enthusiasm.

The prompt spurred a rash of similar greetings from the others. Malini smiled and nodded to be polite.

"Perhaps each of you can demonstrate your gifts. It's customary when Horsemen meet for the first time," Dr. Silva said. "Jacob, you first."

Jacob removed the flask he kept strapped to his ankle and stepped to the center of the room. Into his hand he poured a pillar of water that rotated before freezing and reshaping into a double-edged sword. He maneuvered the weapon around his body so quickly Malini saw only flashes of white. When he'd completed a turn around the room, he tossed the blade into the air. It revolved to the ceiling where it exploded into a billion bits of white.

Snow floated down overhead, fluffy white flakes that settled on everything. Mara caught one in her palm but before she could close her fingers, Jacob whistled. The flake jumped from her hand and flew across the room to Jacob's waiting flask. The remaining flakes followed, until every drop returned to its origin. He screwed the lid back on.

Malini clapped excitedly until she realized she was the only one applauding.

"Nicely done, Jacob," Dr. Silva said. "Lillian?"

In a flash, Lillian dove forward, executing a series of handsprings between the other Horsemen before landing with a short knife in each hand. Malini noticed the sheaths at her thighs, but hadn't seen her draw the weapons. Slicing at the air in a whirlwind of acrobatics, she kicked up a random piece of paper from the desk against the wall. Her knives worked swiftly as it floated to the floor. When she was done, she sheathed the knives and lifted the paper up to the light. In perfectly carved letters it said, *Hello, Mara. Welcome to Paris.*

Malini applauded again. She couldn't help herself. Lillian smiled and nodded in her direction.

"That's cool," Mara said around her sucker. She sounded bored.

"Mara, your turn," Dr. Silva said.

Mara pulled the candy from her mouth and folded it into the saved wrapper. She stuffed it back into her pocket.

Then she disappeared.

"What the hell?" Jacob rushed forward, toward the spot where she'd been.

Malini felt a tap on her shoulder and turned around. Mara stood behind her, close enough that turning had caused her to brush the edge of the new Horseman's open jacket. There was something in her hand, something metal with a wooden handle. Malini tried to see what it was but in the blink of an eye Mara was gone again.

Jacob's laugh brought Malini's attention back to the center of the room. Mara's arm was around his neck, the metal object enclosed in a fist in the center of his back.

"Is it super-speed?" Lillian asked.

"Invisibility?" Jacob guessed.

In a flash, Mara was gone again, reappearing a moment later standing on Dr. Silva's desk. With her hands on her hips, she flashed a smug grin. "Guess again."

The answer popped into Malini's head without any effort on her part. "She's stopping time."

Everyone turned toward Malini.

"How did you figure it out?" Gideon asked in a deep bass that reverberated in the circular room.

Malini rubbed her hands together, uncomfortable with the attention, and tried to answer honestly. "It just popped into my head. But, now that I think about it, I noticed that the papers on the desk didn't move. Invisible or not, if she'd moved fast enough to get across the room that quickly, she would have upset the stack on the corner. She must have got up there carefully, which would have taken time, time she must have made for herself."

Mara retrieved the sucker from her pocket, unwrapped it noisily, and slid it into the side of her mouth. "She's smarter than she looks."

Malini folded her arms against the backhanded compliment.

"How does it work?" Jacob asked, oblivious to the tension between the two girls.

Mara rolled her eyes as if Jacob's question marked him as a complete oaf. She held out her hand. The metal object that Malini glimpsed was cradled in her fingers.

"An enchanted bell?" Jacob asked.

"The bell isn't enchanted, I am," she scoffed. She lowered her chin in Jacob's direction. "Well, if you count being a Horseman enchanted. I can use any bell. It's the act of my ringing it that stops and restarts time."

Malini watched a blush crawl across Jacob's cheeks. Mara had embarrassed him on purpose. Jacob hadn't met any other Horsemen. He didn't know how it worked. It wasn't his fault he thought it was the bell. She suspected Mara enjoyed correcting Jacob. It probably made her feel good about herself.

Worse, she was afraid the blush on Jacob's face was from more than just embarrassment. Malini didn't usually make snap judgments about people, but she didn't like this new Soulkeeper. In fact, at the moment, if Mara had burst into flames, someone else would've had to put her out.

"Something wrong, Malini?" Gideon asked. He'd filed in next to her, following the other Soulkeepers toward the spiral staircase.

Up ahead, Mara walked side by side with Jacob. She was laughing too loudly. Jacob wasn't that funny.

"Look how she touches him every two seconds. What's that all about?" Malini complained.

"It appears Mara is physically attracted to Jacob," Gideon said.

"Thank you, Mr. Obvious. Would you like a spoon to gouge my heart out with?"

"I'm sensing sarcasm in your voice, Malini. Were you expecting me to lie to you? I'm not familiar with all of your human conventions yet. Abigail is much better at untruths than I am."

Malini sighed and stopped Gideon at the top of the stairs. "I don't want you to lie, but some reassurance would be nice."

"He loves you, Malini." Gideon's eyes grew wide with the statement. "Clearly, he does. He does not return her affections."

"Hmph. How do you know for sure? *Look* at her! And she's a Horseman, just like him."

"Beauty is subjective and you are a Soulkeeper of some kind." Gideon laid a hand on her shoulder and her entire body was infused with warmth.

"I'm not. If I were, Dr. Silva would have figured it out by now. Gideon, she doesn't even meet with me anymore. She makes excuse after excuse and is obviously uncomfortable around me. She knows. I'm nothing."

"Sometimes these things happen in their own time. You must not give up. You must trust that you were put here for a reason."

"Really?"

"Yes."

Malini started down the steps. "What you angels fail to admit is sometimes the reason is to take a bullet for someone else."

He nodded in agreement.

"I hate it when you agree with me."

They reached the base of the staircase. Malini was about to jump through the wall when Gideon nudged her arm.

"Malini, remember that I am an angel in love with someone I have never been able to touch, someone I thought was worth … everything. When I came for Abigail, I knew I might be throwing away eternity for the chance at a life I might never earn. How much more must Jacob love you? You, who have proven yourself to be his purpose and his destiny. You, who he can touch and hold. Nothing stands in your way but a few years and your parents' fleeting punishment. Why should you worry?"

Tears welled in Malini's eyes as she thought about the centuries Gideon had waited for Dr. Silva and the day in Nod when Jacob had said he was her destiny, her protector. She thought of the parchment given to her by a Buddhist monk when she was six. On it was the Sanskrit word *apas*, meaning water. The monk told her it was her destiny. She knew now that it meant Jacob.

"You're right," she said. She had no reason to be jealous. She had no reason to be anything but thankful. "Jacob and I were meant for each other. No one can come between us."

Gideon smiled. "Not unless you let them."

He led the way to the other side of the wall.

Chapter 3
The Mission

The group of Soulkeepers moved to the parlor, where Dr. Silva said they would be more comfortable. Certainly the plush seats were better than standing in the tower. She'd brought out some tea and lemonade, along with a tray of cookies that smelled strongly of dark spices. Malini remembered the tea Dr. Silva had made her drink in Nod, how whatever was in it made her heart race like it wanted out of her chest. She decided to stick to the lemonade. Dr. Silva was a whiz at creating herbal concoctions with medicinal properties. Usually she used them for the greater good. Usually.

When they were settled, Dr. Silva spread a newspaper on the coffee table. The headline read: **SERIAL KILLER BAFFLES CHICAGO PD.**

"There's a killer in Chicago," Dr. Silva began. "There've been four deaths so far. The police believe a psychopath is murdering homeless people. We believe there is a Watcher living in the city, feeding in order to stay above ground. Our mission is to find and kill the Watcher before it strikes again."

"How do you know it was a Watcher and not a human murderer?" Jacob asked.

Mara chewed what remained of her sucker and tossed the stick on Dr. Silva's silver tray. "That would be because of me. I live in the area and I felt … drawn to the last kill. I didn't see the killing but when I arrived, the wounds were fresh. The police hadn't been there yet to mess up the scene for me. Every instinct I had told me it was a Watcher. I stopped time and searched for the monster until my power was exhausted but I couldn't find it."

"I thought most Horsemen couldn't sense Watchers?" Malini said.

"They can't," Dr. Silva explained. "But they can sense evil. They are drawn to it like a moth to a flame."

"But what makes you so sure?" Lillian asked Mara. "Instinct can be wrong. If you didn't see it—"

"The flesh had been stripped away," Mara rattled off, "and the throat cut. The police think the throat was cut first and it was rats that ate away the flesh after the death. I was there.

The cuts were clean. The rats came after. Watchers always eat their victims alive. I think the injury on the neck was to cover the marks from crushing his wind pipe so no one could hear him scream."

Malini shuddered in disgust and Jacob placed his hand over hers on her thigh.

"I'm sorry I upset your delicate sensibilities," Mara said through a cynical grin. "Hey, what's your gift anyway, besides emanating super-sweet feminine energy?"

Lillian scooted to the edge of the couch, leaning toward Mara and meeting her eyes. "Mara, I don't know how things are where you come from but here that was incredibly rude. Malini is in transition. She doesn't know what she is yet and she isn't jaded like you are."

Mara didn't apologize. Instead, she locked eyes with Lillian in an unblinking challenge.

"We should have properly introduced Malini upstairs," Dr. Silva said. "Lillian, Mara has been the only Soulkeeper in Chicago for some time. You have to agree that the stress of this find might cause any of us to react in ways we normally wouldn't."

"Of course," Lillian said. She blinked and looked away, effectively ending the stare-off.

Mara fixated on the zipper of her jacket, flipping the silver pull forward and back between her fingers. "I'm sorry," she said toward the floor.

Malini sighed. "It's okay."

Jacob's attention bounced between them like a doubles tennis match. He finally exchanged frustrated looks with Gideon. "So, what can we do? How do we find and stop it?"

"The one thing we can count on is that the Watcher will be lazy and arrogant," Gideon said. "It won't have moved far from the feed, but the illusion it uses will make it hard to find. We'll work in teams. Dr. Silva, Malini, and myself can detect the Watchers. We'll each pair with a Horseman, branching out in separate directions from the site of the murder."

"Wait, I thought you said she was in transition?" Mara said, pointing a hand at Malini. "If Malini's not ready, why are you putting her out front?"

"She can smell Watchers, Mara. We need to use her ability to balance the teams," Dr. Silva responded.

Jacob leapt to his feet. "I agree with Mara. Malini isn't ready. We don't even fully understand what her abilities are. She can't protect herself. It's too dangerous."

"Jacob, don't you think I should make that decision for myself?" Malini said. "Maybe if I'm put in a situation like this it will trigger what I am. I have to be useful for something."

"It's too dangerous!" Jacob insisted, pacing to the gold mantel. A groan came from the pipes as he passed near the wall.

"Please, Jacob—my plumbing. If you're going to have a tantrum, go outside," Dr. Silva said.

Gideon crossed the room and placed a hand on Jacob's shoulder. "It's her purpose, Jacob. Give her the chance to find it, just like you did."

Jacob's hands clenched into fists. He turned to face Malini. "If you're going to do this, do it with me. I want you to be my partner."

"Okay. We'll do this together," Malini said.

"I want Dr. Silva," Mara said. "No way am I charging up Cicero Avenue with super-glow-bright over there."

Gideon scowled. "I will go as the cat. I won't be a danger to anyone."

"Gideon can pair up with me," Lillian said. "I'm not afraid of the Watcher finding us. I want it to find us."

Mara leaned back in her chair and folded her arms across her chest. "It's settled. When do we go?"

"Tomorrow. Sunrise."

Malini exchanged glances with Jacob. It was the weekend, the end of spring break. She didn't have school, but her father wasn't going to make it easy for her to disappear for an entire day. How many more lies could they pile on before they collapsed under their own weight?

Chapter 4
Missing Pieces

As it turned out, Dr. Silva was a huge help in finding an excuse for Malini to be gone all day. She told Mr. Gupta she needed help in her garden and because Jacob, who had worked for her last year, was now working for his uncle at the flower shop, she was willing to pay an embarrassingly high wage for Malini's help. Mr. Gupta, whose weakness was an all-American work ethic, had insisted Malini pick up the extra job.

Malini met the Soulkeepers in the tower, enchanted staff at the ready. Because Mara didn't have a staff, Dr. Silva and Gideon used their sorcery to send her back the way she'd arrived. Once she was safely on the other side, Malini tapped her staff on the floor, producing a loud *crack* like a firecracker that made her ears ring, and a split second later joined the others in an alley near the intersection of Fifth and Cicero.

"This is where it happened." Mara pointed to a patch of pavement near a dumpster. "That building over there—the one with bars on the windows— it's a shelter for the homeless. It was full that night. He'd likely gotten something to eat there, then came here to sleep."

Malini watched the muscles in Mara's cheek tighten as she told the story. Maybe Dr. Silva was right. Maybe the chip on Mara's shoulder was the result of seeing some horrific stuff.

"We should check out the shelter. Ask if anyone saw him that day," Jacob said.

"Good idea," Mara chimed in.

"Wait, you haven't already done that?" Malini asked. "I thought you found him right after it happened? Why wouldn't you have asked some questions then?"

"This place was swarming with cops and news reporters. No way was anyone going to give a kid like me the time of day," Mara said defensively. She shot Malini a deadly glare that seemed to suck all of the oxygen out of the alley.

But it was more than Mara's look that caused Malini to tug at the neck of her hooded jacket. "I feel hot, like I might get sick," she said.

"Malini, is it the Watcher? Can you still smell it here?" Jacob asked.

Nausea often accompanied the noxious odor that told Malini a Watcher was near. She'd noticed it the first time when the Watcher, Auriel, had come to her high school looking for Jacob. Later, she'd guessed Dr. Silva was a fallen angel when her presence produced the same symptoms.

A cool breeze picked up in the alleyway. The air swept away her nausea and cooled her burning skin. She straightened up. "Yes, Jacob. It's been here, but I think not recently. I can only smell it when the wind isn't blowing."

"Yes, I believe you're right, Malini," Dr. Silva said. "Only remnants of evil."

At her feet, Gideon growled in agreement.

"So we search. Give me your staffs. You don't want to call attention to yourselves walking around the city with a tree branch in your hand," Dr. Silva said.

"How do I get one of those anyway?" Mara asked.

"You don't," Malini quipped in a not-so-nice way.

"Malini—" Jacob started.

Dr. Silva saved him from finishing the statement. "Mara, the staffs were made from the branches of a tree that grew out of my dead husband. Sorry, but his soul has moved on, the tree is dead, and we can't make any more."

Mara blinked several times in Dr. Silva's direction. "Makes ... perfect ... sense," she said, raising an eyebrow. Absently, she reached into her coat and withdrew another sucker, yanking off the paper cover and thrusting it into her cheek.

Malini, Jacob, and Lillian added their staffs to the two already in Dr. Silva's arms. She leaned them up against the dumpster. With a deliberate flourish, her hands circled her body, pulling the air into a glowing orb that burned like fire but crackled like electricity. When the magic was the size of a soccer ball, Dr. Silva tossed the flames at the stack and the staffs melted from view.

"This cloaking illusion will last only two hours. We'll need to split up. Mara and I will investigate the shelter. I wouldn't put it past a Watcher to pose as another homeless person. Lillian, you and Gideon go north. Jacob and Malini, south." Dr. Silva motioned toward the mouth of the alley.

"Let's do this thang," Mara said, following her lead.

Malini nodded her head. Weird, a quiet voice at the back of her skull was telling her to go south, anyway. She hoped the voice was her instinct guiding her away from the evil. Unlike Lillian, Malini didn't want to be the one to find the Watcher.

"Come on," Jacob said to her. "Tell me if the smell gets stronger."

The two broke away from the rest of the group, moving out of the alley and strolling side by side down Cicero Avenue. Traffic was dense, but luckily, the drivers seemed preoccupied with their own business. Jacob was in full Horseman mode, sweeping each passerby for any glimpse of suspicious activity. Malini, on the other hand, wasn't thinking about their mission. She watched her shoes hit the pavement, completely distracted.

"Jacob, do you think Mara is attractive?"

"Sure. I guess," he answered without looking at her.

"What is it about her that you find attractive?"

This second question grabbed Jacob's attention more than the first. He turned toward Malini and frowned.

"I didn't say I was attracted to her, specifically. I said she was attractive in a general sense."

"Well, what do you think is attractive about her in a general sense, then?"

Jacob opened and closed his mouth. "Malini, I don't think I should answer that question."

"Well, why not?"

"Yesterday, you and Mara didn't really hit it off. No plans for a new BFF there I would say. So, I'm afraid my words can and will be used against me."

"So, you do find her attractive."

"Will you stop saying the word *attractive* like you looked it up in a thesaurus under 'ambiguous words to trap your boyfriend with?'"

"Just answer the question."

"See, this is what I'm talking about. You're leading me into something, Malini. What is it that you want me to say?"

Malini crossed her arms in a huff and walked faster. "If I tell you what I want you to say, it's not worth hearing you say it," she blurted.

"I see. So, either you're digging for a compliment or trying to trap me into saying I find Mara attractive." He laughed. He actually laughed at her.

Malini rushed ahead. She refused to look at him even though a small part of her knew he might be right.

"Malini, if you want me to reassure you—" His arm shot out in front of her. She halted abruptly, swerving to avoid him. His other arm shot out behind her, corralling her on the square of sidewalk. She ducked under it. He surrounded her again with lightning-fast reflexes. His bright green eyes smoldered above his teasing grin.

She refused to look at him. Retreating from his arms, she backed into the privacy fence that bordered the sidewalk. He moved in close, his hands coming to rest on the fence on either side of her shoulders.

"If you want me to reassure you, Malini, all you have to do is ask," he said softly. His leg slipped between hers until his knee hit the wood behind her. Bending his elbows, he pressed into her. He wasn't laughing anymore.

As Malini turned the full force of her deadliest look in his direction, Jacob lowered his lips onto hers. Soft at first, a mere brush of lip to lip, the kiss was an appeal for permission. She acquiesced, parting her lips. The kiss deepened, igniting a slow burn that threatened to start the fence on fire.

They were both sixteen, but becoming a Horseman had matured Jacob. He was all muscle and almost a foot taller than her. His body engulfed Malini's as he bent his neck to kiss her again. Every nerve ending woke up and sent little shock waves to the deepest part of her. Her skin flushed. Her heart pounded.

She was so caught up in the kiss, she almost didn't notice the smell. The first licks of it came on a breeze, making her pull back a little. The second, stronger, caused her to push hard against Jacob's chest. She turned her head and inhaled the sickeningly foul smell of Watcher, a metallic sweetness like arsenic and aspartame.

"It's here," she whispered into Jacob's ear and pointed her thumb behind her. "I think, behind the fence."

He was gone in a flash, the warmth of his body replaced with cool spring air. She tried to follow, but she wasn't nearly as fast. Yards ahead of her, he turned the corner. She caught up to him where the eight-foot wooden slats gave way to chain link. The entrance gate was chained shut.

"A junkyard," she said, panting. "No attendant on duty. How do we get in?"

"*We* don't. You need to stay here where it's safe." Jacob pulled up his pant leg and removed the flask of water that was strapped to his ankle. Filled with holy water, the flask was a Christmas gift from his mom. He never left home without it. "I'll go over alone. I can take this thing."

The top of the fence was lined with barbed wire. Visions of Jacob bloodied and tangled in its barbs danced through Malini's head. There had to be another way.

"Break the lock, Jacob. Don't go over. Someone driving by might see." She pulled out her cell phone, her thumbs flying across the keyboard. "I've texted the others. Help is coming."

"I can't wait. I understand what Mara was talking about now when she said she was drawn to it. My body is about to pull a sucker-punch on my brain and drag my hijacked ass in there. Besides, we can't give it a chance to get away."

At least he listened to her about the fence. He lifted the padlock in his hand and filled the mechanism with water, maintaining contact so that it wouldn't drip through his fingers. He froze the liquid, spreading the ice where the key should have been. The lock opened.

"Go ahead, Jacob. I'll close it behind you," Malini said.

He slipped through and disappeared behind stacks of tires and rows of rusted cars. Malini did as she promised. She closed and locked the gate behind him, but not before she slid through into the junkyard. There was no way she was going to leave him to do this alone. Dr. Silva would make short work of the lock anyway.

"Solve the problem," she said to herself. That was what her father always told her. It was all about critical thinking. Plan the work then work the plan. She didn't know what she was or what power she had, but today, even if she was an ordinary girl, she was going to help Jacob kill this Watcher.

She scanned the junk in front of her. *Up,* she thought. She needed to climb higher. With a bird's eye view, she'd be in a better position to help Jacob. A boxcar rusting in the west corner caught her eye. *Perfect.*

On quiet feet, she ran as fast as she could to the wreck and climbed the ladder up the side. Thankfully, from her perch on the boxcar roof, she could see most of the junkyard. Stacked vehicles blocked the southwest corner, but otherwise, the twisted metal was low enough to provide an unhindered view. She found Jacob right away, creeping forward between stacks of junk, holding tight to one side of the path.

Unfortunately, she spotted the Watcher next. The sight of it made her gag. It wore the illusion of a young man in overalls, a form that fit right in with the surroundings. Anyone who caught a glimpse from the outside would think he was a custodian. But Malini knew what he was immediately. His smell rose up over the rest of the rot and hit her full force in the face. If that wasn't enough of a clue, the Watcher was eating something, and from where she stood, it looked a lot like a human foot.

Malini whipped her phone from her pocket. *Left,* she texted to Jacob's number.

She watched him pull his phone from his pocket to silence the vibration.

Where R U, he texted back.

Never mind. Go left.

Jacob moved forward and followed her directions, circling around a pyramid of stacked barrels, low and out of sight.

Left again. Right after the blue Nova. Careful, U R close.

He followed her directions, creeping down the pathway and then sliding around the blue car at the end. The Watcher stopped eating and sniffed the air, tossing the bones he'd been chewing aside and wiping the blood from his hands on his overalls. Malini saw the smear for only a moment and then it faded into the illusion, swallowed by the fake perfection Watchers liked to use.

It senses U, Malini texted, but it was too late. The Watcher spotted Jacob's feet under the Nova and instantly transformed itself into a little girl in a pink dress and pigtails.

Girl is Watcher! Malini typed frantically.

She was too late. Jacob had already stowed his phone in order to pour the water from his flask into his palm. His favorite broadsword of ice formed in his hand and he crouched into a fighting stance.

As Malini feared, he hesitated when the little girl scampered around the corner.

"Help me," the girl said, holding out a chubby hand.

"What are you doing in here?" Jacob asked.

Malini said a silent prayer that Jacob wouldn't lower his weapon. The little girl inched closer, her eyes as big as saucers, her chubby hand reaching for Jacob's. And Jacob was reaching back, drawn in by the illusion. Malini had to do something. She had to warn him.

"*Jacob, it's her!*" Malini screamed.

Jacob leapt back and wielded his weapon. The little girl façade ripped in half and the black scaly skin of a Watcher emerged. Leathery wings sprung forth with a menacing hiss. Dodging Jacob's thrust, it lunged a taloned paw at his stomach, ripping through sweatshirt and flesh. Blood soaked the cotton. Jacob slashed and dove, avoiding the beast's claws. Somersaulting between its legs, his second jab landed in the creature's thigh. The holy water of the blade burned its flesh. The creature howled.

From her position, Malini lost sight of Jacob. He'd rolled behind the scrap, out of view. She'd need to climb higher to make sure he was okay. Unfortunately, that plan would have to wait. A more pressing problem required her immediate attention.

Below her, a second Watcher approached the boxcar. It stared up at her, squinting its snake-like yellow eyes. She'd learned in Nod that, whatever she was, she was hard for Watchers to see. But she was sure she was easy for them to hear, and her scream had just given away her location.

Backing away from the edge as quietly as possible, she dropped down on the opposite side, hiding in the shadow of twisted rubbish. The puncture of metal gave her goose bumps as the Watcher clawed its way up the side of the boxcar. The monster scuffled across the top and then a winged shadow crept over her, blocking out the sun.

She bolted, launching herself between piles of junk and ducking behind the first mass of metal big enough to hide her. It was a mistake. The pebbles and dust she kicked up only drew attention to her location. Behind her, wings flapped and footsteps pounded the dirt, closer and closer. Pulse racing, head filled with visions of Nod, she lost all control and panicked. She raced for the gate. The beast was on her in an instant, its serpentine hands snatching her backward by the jacket.

Malini's head snapped forward from the jolt. The beast whipped her around. Talons. Scales. Foul breath. Sharp teeth. Its yellow eyes drew ever closer. Losing all capability for logical thought, she became a whirlwind of biting teeth and scratching nails. She wriggled from her jacket, freeing herself to take a few more running steps. The Watcher pounced, gripping her shoulders. She kicked and thrashed. A terror-fueled shriek worthy of any horror movie escaped her throat.

And then a miracle happened. The place where the Watcher's black scaly hands touched her bare skin, beneath the cap sleeves of her T-shirt, began to burn. Agonizing pain radiated through Malini's shoulders. The Watcher must have felt it too because it snatched its taloned paws away, shaking them. Had it burned her or had she burned it? Malini didn't wait to find out.

Kicking hard against the Watcher's ribs, she freed herself, falling to the dirt in the process. She crab-walked away from the beast, unable to find her footing.

"What are you?" the Watcher growled, paws covered in blisters. So was the skin on her upper arms where it had touched her.

It didn't take long for the creature to figure out another way. With an evil smile, it ripped a pronged chunk of steel from the rubbish and stabbed it at her with supernatural precision. It caught her around the neck and fixed her to the earth. Helpless, Malini struggled, a butterfly stuck with a pin.

The Watcher closed in. Something sharp glinted from the creature's talons. A knife. *Where did it get a knife?*

"See you in Hell, whatever you are," the Watcher said, raising the blade over her heart.

"I don't think so." Jacob's foot barreled into the Watcher's side. They tumbled to her left in the dirt. She tried to watch but the cold steel that scraped the sides of her neck wouldn't allow her to turn her head. She heard thrashing, a grunt, and then Jacob howled in pain.

Malini couldn't bear it. She closed her eyes and prepared herself for the end, praying in her last moments for Jacob's safety. But, a split second later, instead of death, familiar voices came for her. Inexplicably, the metal prong was gone and she rubbed her scraped neck in relief.

"It's okay, Malini. I'm here." Jacob scooped her trembling body into his arms and stood her up next to him.

The Watcher was pinned to the earth, electric purple energy binding its arms, legs, and wings. *When had that happened?* Mara, Gideon, and Lillian looked on as Dr. Silva lowered a glowing purple spear toward the creature's heart.

"Why did you come here?" she demanded.

The beast gave a wicked laugh that made the hair on Malini's neck stand on end. She hugged tighter to Jacob's chest.

"Your partner is already dead. Tell us why you came and we may spare you," Dr. Silva said again.

"Why?" the thing laughed. "You ask why? The why is already done. We are everywhere, traitor. And you..." Its yellow eyes washed over each of them. "None of you are safe. We know who you are, and we know how to find you. We will be avenged, Soulkeepers. The next flood is coming. This time it will be Watchers on the ark and the righteous shall perish." The beast laughed sardonically until Dr. Silva plunged her weapon into its chest. The flesh imploded, folding inward before turning to ash. They all stared at the place where it had been, the cremated remains blending into the dirt pathway.

Jacob groaned and clutched his side.

"Let me get that for you," Gideon said. He placed a hand over Jacob's stomach wound. The bleeding stopped and the skin healed to a pale pink.

"Thanks," Jacob said.

Gideon noticed Malini's upper arms next. "You've been hit with its energy. These burns run deep." He held her wounds until the burns healed. It was a long wait.

"Thanks, Gideon," Malini murmured. Physically, she was healed, but inside she felt shaken to the core.

If the experience with the Watcher fazed Mara at all, there was no telling from the outside. She hadn't even broken a sweat. Catching Malini's eye, she held up her bell and gave a half grin. "You can thank me later."

Chapter 5
Doubts

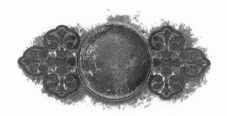

They arrived at Dr. Silva's in silence, Malini clinging to Jacob as if he were a buoy in an ocean that threatened to gobble her up. Maybe she *was* drowning. She couldn't catch her breath. Her heart raced under her clammy skin, and her whole body trembled.

"It's okay, Malini." Jacob stroked her hair. "We're back. You're okay. Nothing is going to hurt you here."

Dr. Silva put a hand on her shoulder. "I'm sorry to interrupt but I think you'd better go. I told your father you'd be home by dinner."

Malini slid from Jacob's arms, waiting until the last moment to relinquish his fingers.

"Do you want me to come with you?" Jacob asked.

"You can't, Jacob. I'm grounded from you, remember?" With short goodbyes to the rest of the team, she followed Dr. Silva to the door. Jacob trailed close behind. At the look of concern on his face, she said, "Don't worry. I can drive myself home. I'm fine."

Dr. Silva handed her a fifty-dollar bill. "Your wages."

"Are you sure?"

"We have to make this seem realistic. Your father will know if I don't pay you."

"Yes, of course." Malini took the bill and slid it into her pocket, then walked toward her car parked in the driveway. She climbed behind the wheel and backed out onto Rural Route One. She drove into town on autopilot, allowing her brain to wander to a place of blank indifference. If she didn't think about anything, she could handle this.

But when she passed McNaulty's restaurant, visions of the Watcher, Auriel, chased away her numb peace. Auriel had been here last year. Watchers *could* come to Paris. They could be here right now.

Her hands gripped the steering wheel tighter, her knuckles turning white. She waited at Paris' only traffic light and wondered if she would ever feel safe again.

A knock on her window made her jump. Her foot slid from the brake and her car lurched forward before she was able to reposition herself. Dane stood at the window, his hands raised on either side of his shoulders.

"I'm sorry!" he said through the glass. "I didn't mean to scare you."

Things had changed since Dane had a run in with Auriel that almost cost him his life. He was her friend now, and Malini was painfully aware that he was the only one in Paris who might understand what she was going through. She rolled down the window.

"Hey, Dane. What's up?"

"Nothing. I was just heading to McNaulty's to see if you and Jacob were there and saw you stopped at a green light. By the way, you just about hit the roof."

Malini pursed her lips and searched Dane's gray eyes. "I have to go home for dinner but there's something I want to talk to you about. Can you come by my house later? In like an hour?"

Dane placed both hands on the passenger side door and poked his head into her window. His face paled and his expression melted into apprehension. "Is this about what I think it's about?"

"Yes."

"I'll be there."

The light was green again. "Later, then," she said and shifted her attention to the road. In the back of her mind, she wondered if Jacob would be okay with her talking to Dane about what happened. But, as she saw it, she didn't have a choice. Jacob wasn't allowed near her house and she had to talk to someone. If she held what she was feeling inside, she would explode. As it was, she wondered if she would ever sleep again.

* * * * *

"This is what I've been talking about, Malini. If you apply yourself, you could save enough money to cover your college living expenses. The tuition is only half the battle." Malini's father held up the fifty-dollar bill before rising from the table and adding it to a glass jar on the kitchen counter. He returned to the table looking proud. "I knew this break from Jacob would be beneficial for you."

Malini was incensed. "Daddy, Jacob was the reason I was able to get both jobs. His uncle owns Laudner's Flowers and he put in a good word for me with Dr. Silva. If anything, he's been a good influence."

"A good influence? You think driving you across the country without our permission is a good influence?"

Malini raged internally at the lie they'd chosen to tell to cover their visit to Nod. It was the type of lie you thought you could tell once and be done with it, but she was beginning to think her father would never let go of this particular mistake.

"We've been over this. It was my idea. Jacob just went along. Besides, it was meant to be. If we'd never taken the trip we would've never found Lillian."

"Don't justify your mistakes with convenient coincidences, Malini. I don't believe for a second Jacob wasn't the cause of your behavior. We didn't raise you to be so reckless."

Mrs. Gupta, who had remained silent up to this point, seemed to notice the tension at the table had reached critical proportions. "I will not allow this fighting at my table. It is disrespectful to me."

Malini and her father looked down at their plates. They finished their meal in the sort of silence that rattled through all of them as loudly as a scream.

She'd just finished clearing the table when the doorbell rang.

"Who the hell could that be?" her father said, moving toward the door. As Malini rinsed the plates and placed them in the dishwasher, she could hear the door swing open. Dane's voice cut through the room.

"Hi. You must be Mr. Gupta. I'm Dane. I go to school with Malini. I was wondering if she was home and, if so, if I could speak with her for a moment?"

Malini grinned at the ridiculous level of politeness. Dane was laying it on thick.

There was a pause, then her father seemed to find his voice. "Of course, Dane, it is a pleasure to meet you. Let me go get her."

The sound of Dane's feet echoing in the marble foyer raised Malini's spirits. She met her father as he entered the kitchen. He seemed pleased, probably because Dane wasn't Jacob. The thought made Malini roll her eyes.

"You have a visitor," her father said.

"Thanks," Malini murmured. She didn't make eye contact. She ducked around her father's body and met Dane in the foyer.

"Hey," she said. "Is it nice outside?"

"If you consider nice forty-four degrees and drizzling."

"Nice enough. Do you want to take a walk?"

"Sure."

Malini yelled behind her to her parents, her voice echoing through the two-story foyer. "I'm going for a walk."

"Okay," her mother called. Malini heard her father chide her mother for the approval but she lifted her North Face from the hook and exited the house before her mom could rescind her permission. She strode up the driveway, Dane trailing behind.

"Your dad seems nice," Dane said.

"He's being an ass-hat."

"Ooookay."

"Seriously, I've been grounded from Jacob since the end of October. He's my boyfriend, Dane. It's totally unfair."

At the end of the driveway, she slowed her pace. The pebbles on the side of the road crunched under her feet. "So, was that what you wanted to talk to me about?" Dane asked.

"No." Malini looked over her shoulder at the row of suburban houses that included her own. They were alone. "There was a mission today. I went. I saw two Watchers just like Auriel. One almost killed me."

Dane doubled over, resting his hands on his knees. He took long deep breaths through his mouth like he'd just been clubbed in the stomach. "Are they coming here?"

"No. Dane, they're dead. Jacob killed one and Dr. Silva killed the other. But it had me. It was close and it didn't want to capture me. It wanted me dead."

Slowly, he stood up and started walking again. He'd pulled himself together but his face was still white as death against his black wool coat. "I have nightmares, Malini. Last year ... I've thought about it a lot and it was like I couldn't make my own decisions while I was with Auriel."

"It was the tea, Dane. You were basically drugged. It wasn't your fault. You didn't know what she was."

"That's true but the scary part is, sometimes I miss it."

"Miss it? What the tea?"

"No ... Yes." He mimicked balancing scales with his hands. "It wasn't the tea exactly. It was the way I felt powerful when I was with her. I felt like I could do anything. I could have anything I wanted. I felt really good about myself."

"And you don't now?"

"Not like that. Now, I feel normal. I know I can do things, be somebody, but I have to do it the hard way. College..." He shook his head.

"I know. I mean, I think I know what you are feeling. I stared evil in the face this morning. I'm not exactly focused on what I want to be when I grow up."

"It's not just that. I'm supposed to take over the family farm. Corn and soybeans—it's who we are. What the hell is the point of me going to college? I don't have a choice of what I'm going to be, anyway. When I was with Auriel, drinking her tea, I didn't care. I was ready to tell my dad he could shove it. Now? I care. I know what the farm means to him and I'm afraid that guilt is going to keep me here forever."

"Wow, Dane, I never realized you felt that way."

"Well, you're the first person I've actually told. I mean, it's not like I can tell just anyone about Auriel and everyone else in this town thinks I've got it made. We own the richest farm in Paris."

They'd reached the end of her cul-de-sac where a quaint neighborhood park nestled between the maple trees. She passed the slide and picnic table and sat down on one of two swings near the back. Dane sat in the other.

"I don't know what I am, Dane."

"You mean, like, you don't know what you're going to be? You could be anything, Malini. You're the smartest person I know."

"No, that's not what I mean. Jacob was able to fight off Auriel and get you help because he's a Soulkeeper. He's genetically gifted to fight Watchers. Dr. Silva is his Helper—like a trainer or coach that helps him do his job."

"Well, that explains a lot."

"Yeah, I know we never talk about this outright, but I need to. See, I thought I was different, too. I could smell

Auriel so Dr. Silva thought I might be some sort of Soulkeeper. But I've been experimenting for months and no one knows what I am. I was almost killed today because I'm playing at being a part of this when really, I'm just a regular person caught up in this nightmare."

"Like me."

"Yes, like you. All I want to do is have a normal life. You said you have nightmares. I have nightmares, too. Today, I lived a major nightmare. I love Jacob, but this is too much."

Dane pushed against the dirt and swung on the swing a few times. "Do you ever wish you were a little kid again and your biggest worry was what your mom was going to make for lunch?"

Malini pushed off next to him, pumping her legs. Dane followed her lead. She pointed her toes toward the sky, like she used to do when she was a kid, as if she could stab a cloud with her toe and bring it down to Earth. When she rose above the bar and the seat dropped abruptly, she laughed at the feeling and allowed herself to slump in her swing until it slowed. Dane dragged his feet and came to a stop next to her. He reached over and wrapped his gloved hand around hers on the chain.

"Malini, I don't know anything about being a Soulkeeper, but you are different. You're smart, and fun, and a hell of a good listener."

His eyes dwelled on hers. Malini shifted on her swing and pulled her hand from his grasp. "You're a good friend, too,

Dane." She took a few steps toward the road. "We should head back. It's getting dark."

Dane retracted the hand that had held Malini's. He stood from his seat on the swing and followed her to the road. They walked back in silence, reaching her driveway just as the setting sun cast an orangey-purple glow across the horizon.

"Thanks, Dane, for being here for me. I guess the upside of all of this is we have each other. We may not be part of this war between the Soulkeepers and the Watchers, but we can help each other get through it."

"Amen to that, sister," Dane said with a smile.

Malini waved goodbye as he climbed into his car and pulled out of her driveway.

Chapter 6
Debriefing

After Malini left Dr. Silva's, Jacob returned to the parlor and sat down next to his mother. Gideon paced and the rest of the room was just as fidgety.

"What does it mean? What do you think they were doing above ground?" Lillian asked.

Jacob held up a hand. "The question isn't what were they doing, but what had they done? The Watcher said it was done. It said none of us were a secret anymore and the next flood would 'end the righteous.'" He flexed his fingers to put air quotes around the last part for emphasis.

"But what does it mean?" Mara asked. "The Watcher said it knew who we were. How can that be?"

"It could've been lying," Jacob offered.

"But what if it wasn't? What if I've been outed? I have to live there. I'm by myself. I'll be dead before you can say, 'Beware of the Watcher.'"

"I'm not sure what it means," Dr. Silva said. "It could be a lie but I don't think we can take that chance. I think you should stay here, Mara, until we know for sure."

"But what about your family?" Jacob asked.

"Don't have any worth mentioning. My parental units and I don't see eye to eye. They still live in Florida. We haven't spoken in over a year." She turned toward Dr. Silva. "I work as a nursing assistant. Do you think you can come up with some sort of excuse for me?"

"Consider it done. You can stay with Gideon and me until we figure this out. No Watcher would be bold enough to try for you here."

"How do we figure out the rest of it?" Mara asked.

"The rest of what?" Jacob asked.

"At the shelter, we found out the victim's name was Frank. Turns out he's not the first shelter patron to go missing. You should have seen the bulletin board. They've lost track of twenty-five in the last year," Mara explained.

"Shit, do you think Watchers took them all?"

"Maybe."

"But Frank was only the second found dead. Where are the rest of the bodies? Do you think they've taken them all to Nod?"

"We don't know, Jacob, but it's suspicious. We need to talk to the Healer. Until then we'll watch the papers. They have to be getting help from this side, a leader of some sort, someone with influence. We'll watch for the signs."

"Signs? What signs?" Lillian asked.

"A person corrupted by the Watchers changes, Lillian. They'll start making mistakes, losing their temper, making poor choices. Perhaps you remember a certain Hollywood starlet who attacked her assistant last fall? Out of character and an almost certain sign she'd been influenced by the Watchers."

"So, we're looking for someone who acts out violently," Lillian said.

"Or without compassion," Gideon added.

The room plunged into silence, each Soulkeeper finding a separate spot in the room to absorb their thoughts. The sound of Mara chewing the last broken bits of her sucker broke the funeral parlor ambience.

"We'd better go, Jacob. The Laudners are going to wonder where we are," Lillian said. She smoothed her hair and tightened her ponytail. "I think Katrina came home today. They're going to want to go out to dinner."

Jacob rolled his eyes but followed her lead toward the door, nodding his goodbyes along the way.

"Enjoy the family feedbag," Mara yelled sarcastically.

"Mara!" Dr. Silva said.

"What?" Mara asked.

Jacob exited the Victorian and crossed the street to the Laudners' cheery yellow home. His mom opened the door, straight into a heated conversation between Aunt Carolyn and Katrina.

"What do you mean, you don't remember?" Aunt Carolyn yelled, then seemed to notice him and his mom standing in the doorway. "Hello," she said briskly.

"Hello. Welcome home, Katrina," Lillian said. "Is everything okay?"

"Fine," Aunt Carolyn said. "Only, my daughter won't share a single thing about this semester. From her grades to what she did last night, I get no information."

"I don't want to talk about it," Katrina said. She looked tired and held her head in her hands like every spoken word pounded against her skull.

"Stop the bullshit, Katrina. You're hung over," Aunt Carolyn said. She turned her attention to Lillian and Jacob. "Sorry you had to see this. We thought we would all go to Andrew's Steak House for dinner. That is, if my daughter can hold her head up for the hour while we eat."

Katrina rolled her eyes and shifted her gaze toward Jacob. They'd never been chummy, but the look she gave him bordered on deadly. Jacob wouldn't give her the satisfaction of wallowing in her death rays. He climbed the stairs to his room, locking his door behind him.

* * * * *

In his blue rust-bucket truck, Jacob followed the Laudners' Ford Focus to Andrew's Steakhouse on the edge of Route 9. His mom rode shotgun. Technically, they could've all fit in one car, but they'd be packed in like sardines. He'd offered to drive separately. Thanks to his mom backing that idea up, the Laudners didn't say no.

"Katrina looks…" His mom shook her head.

"Like crap?" Jacob filled in.

"I think there's a more polite word for it but she doesn't look good."

"Heavy night of partying, I guess." Jacob pulled onto the gravel parking lot in front of the painted blue wood panel of Andrew's and parked near the front door.

"It seems weird. She knew she was coming home today."

"People her age drink, Mom. She's nineteen; she's away at school. She got drunk."

"Well, I'm going to offer to sleep on the couch tonight. I know it stresses her out to share a room with me."

"I can sleep on the couch. You can have my room."

She smiled in his direction. "That's sweet, Jacob, but honestly, I don't mind. And I want to extend the olive branch to her. If you do it, it won't mean the same thing."

Jacob frowned but nodded. They climbed out of the truck, slamming the doors behind them. Jacob didn't bother locking it. The population of Paris was just over three thousand. If it were stolen it wouldn't take much investigation to find the culprit. On the off chance an outsider drove the hundred miles to come to Paris to steal a car, he suspected it wouldn't be his dumpy blue truck.

They joined the Laudners at the door. The smell of grilling meat and grease hit him head-on as he entered the wood-paneled glory that was Andrew's Steakhouse. They were seated at a large round table. Instinctively, Jacob took a seat next to his mom and was surprised when Katrina flopped into a chair next to him.

He turned his face toward his mom and murmured under his breath, "Huh." Katrina never voluntarily sat next to Jacob … ever.

"She's in trouble. You're the other kid in the household. It's only natural," his mom whispered with a hard undercurrent of *be polite*.

He looked straight ahead, toward the waitress who'd approached the table. Katrina's cold, dark stare burrowed into the side of his head.

"What'll it be, hon?" the waitress asked him.

"Um, the sirloin, medium," Jacob said.

"And you," she said turning to Katrina.

"The Branson rib eye, rare."

"Katrina, that's a twenty-eight ounce piece of meat and you've never liked your steak rare. Stop messing around and order something you're actually going to eat," John said.

"I changed my mind. I like my steak rare now and I'm really hungry. Isn't this a welcome home dinner for me?" she countered.

"You know what? Fine. I suppose they can throw it back on the grill if they need to."

Katrina leaned into her chair, a smug half-smile creeping across her face. As much as Jacob thought he had hated her before, there was something more sinister about Katrina this time. She'd changed and he didn't think it was for the better.

When the food came, the waitress set what looked like half a cow in front of Katrina. It was barely brown on the outside and bled across the plate when she cut into it. Everyone stared at her as she ate her first bite.

"What?" she asked.

Uncle John changed the subject. "Did you hear about Stephanie Westcott?"

"What about her?" Lillian asked.

"She's missing. Was supposed to come home from school today and never showed up. Fran Westcott is beside herself."

"What about her roommate?" Jacob asked, his fork and knife poised over his steak.

"She says she left Indiana University yesterday morning," Carolyn said. "They've called the police and everything."

Lillian placed her hand on her chest. "How horrible. Any chance this might be a social thing? Taking off with a friend for spring break?"

"We can only hope." Carolyn's eyes darted accusingly in Jacob's direction, an obvious jab about his supposed joyride with Malini last year.

"Who the hell cares," Katrina said, forking in another bite of steak.

"Katrina!" Carolyn gasped.

"Oh, come on, Mom, like you ever said 'boo' to Stephanie Westcott. Besides sucking down Fran Westcott's blueberry pie at every church social, you have no relationship."

"Don't you think that's a little callus?" Lillian said.

"Whatever." Katrina chugged her water.

"The least we can do is pray for her safe return. Carolyn, maybe you and I could offer to bring by some meals. I'm sure with the stress, Fran isn't eating well," Lillian said.

Katrina snorted. "Have you *seen* Fran Westcott? That woman has never missed a meal."

Uncle John grunted. "That's enough, Katrina."

Lillian furrowed her brow in Jacob's direction. He shrugged and returned to his plate, taking a bite of his steak. The table grew quiet aside from the clink of silverware. The pause in conversation allowed his mind to wander and his thoughts marched directly back to Malini.

He wondered how she was doing. He'd never seen her so upset. He couldn't blame her. She was thrown into all of this with no proof that she was really ready. Maybe she did have a gift that would surface at any moment. Maybe she didn't. Either way she wasn't ready for the kind of confrontation that happened today. Malini had seen Nod. She'd seen the way the Watchers there tortured human souls. He couldn't imagine how terrifying it must have been for her to be pinned to the dirt like some kind of animal, knowing that her life could end in a heartbeat. And wasn't he a wuss to not follow her home? That's what he should have done. If he was any sort of a boyfriend he would have followed at a distance and made sure she got home okay.

"Are you finished? Do you want a box?" the waitress asked.

He'd been so caught up in his thoughts about Malini he hadn't noticed that everyone else was done eating. Half his steak remained on his plate. "Yeah, a box would be great," he replied.

The woman tucked her pen behind her ear and lifted his plate in one hand and Katrina's in the other. That's when Jacob noticed her plate was empty. In surprise, he looked over at her just in time to watch her lick a bit of blood from her lips.

"I guess you were hungry," he said.

"Yeah, like I said." She leaned back in her chair.

Uncle John paid the check and they filed out into the parking lot. "Maybe, I could ride with you, Jacob?" Katrina said. Her voice was too sweet, poisoned honey.

"Sorry, no space. There's not much room in the cab and my mom is riding home with me."

"Maybe she could go with Mom and Dad," Katrina said.

"Uh…" Jacob tried to think of some excuse to put her off. Luckily, Lillian came to the rescue.

"I get car sick riding in the backseat. I better stick with Jacob."

Katrina's eyes darkened. "Fine," she said. She backed away, only breaking eye contact when she'd reached the car.

Jacob and Lillian climbed into the truck. As soon as the doors were closed, Jacob couldn't keep it in any longer. "There's something wrong with Katrina. I can feel it."

"I sense it, too," Lillian said. "I don't need Malini to know she reeks of Watcher."

"Do you think she met one at school? Maybe she's been influenced," Jacob said.

"I don't know, but we can't trust her until we figure it out," Lillian replied. "I'm going to see if I can get my hands on her phone and check her records. If a Watcher is manipulating her, it will have to meet with her regularly to maintain its influence."

"Auriel only visited Dane once a month."

Lillian turned surprised eyes toward him. "What?"

"He told me she would leave a thermos full of tea. That's how she got him, with the tea."

"We need to look for a source. Something she's taking in. Until then don't trust her," Lillian said.

"I didn't trust her before," Jacob said. "Maybe it's a good thing you're sleeping on the couch tonight."

"And maybe you should lock your door."

Silence crept between them, as thoughts of Watchers, Katrina, and what was to come drained any hope of lighter conversation.

* * * * *

It was late by the time they returned home, which was good because it gave Jacob a reason to avoid Katrina. He ascended the stairs and locked the door to his room behind him just as his mother requested. But he had no intention of going to sleep. Malini must be a basket case by now and he wasn't going to leave her alone a minute longer. Besides, if Katrina was being influenced by a Watcher, that was information Malini needed to know.

He retrieved his staff from his closet but knew he couldn't use it immediately. The staffs made a sound like a firecracker when used, and he didn't want to call attention to his departure. It was inconvenient, but when he stopped to think about his molecules being channeled through the air to somewhere else, it seemed only fitting that the process happened with a bang.

To be safe, he formed his pillows and blankets into a Jacob-sized heap on the bed. The old-fashioned lock on the door wasn't exactly foolproof and the Laudners had a key. If they came in, it wouldn't hurt to have a decoy.

An old pull string bag made an excellent sling for the staff. He loaded it onto his back and carefully climbed out the window. Perching on the rose trellis, he slid the glass panel closed behind him. He descended on shaky toes and jogged quietly from the house. When he was a respectable distance, he stopped, concentrated on Malini's terrace, and tapped the staff on the concrete.

Jacob arrived outside Malini's window. For a moment he held perfectly still, hoping he hadn't woken her parents or a neighbor. Once he'd determined all was quiet, he knocked lightly on her window. The lace curtain moved aside.

Malini's face lit up when she saw him and she unlocked her window to welcome him inside.

"I'm so glad you came," she said, folding herself against his chest.

"I've been thinking about you since you left Dr. Silva's. I had to make sure you were okay."

Malini walked over to her bed and sat down near the pillow, pulling her legs up underneath her. She wore a butter-yellow T-shirt and some flowered shorts Jacob knew she slept in. Without a hint of makeup and her hair loose around her shoulders, Jacob thought she was the most beautiful thing he'd ever seen. He crossed the room and took a seat on the bed next to her.

"I wasn't okay when I got here, but I'm doing better now. I had a talk with a friend and I realized that what I'm feeling is perfectly natural considering the circumstances."

The muscles of Jacob's shoulders and neck tightened. "What friend?" he asked.

"Dane."

A red tide washed over Jacob, a feeling of possessiveness that he didn't quite understand. "Dane?"

"Yes, I ran into him on the way home. I needed someone to talk to and he's the only other person who knows about the Watchers."

"I'm not sure it's a good idea to trust Dane, Malini. He's been manipulated by the Watchers before."

"That's precisely why I do trust him. You should see how upset he was when he heard what happened. He fears them as much as we do, Jacob. He would be the last one to allow himself to be manipulated by one."

"Huh," Jacob said. He'd like to think the frown he gave her was out of genuine concern for her safety but part of him could feel the jealousy lurking behind it. "So, tell me what you and Dane talked about."

"Dane and I are the same. We're a part of this now because we know about the Watchers but we're not really Soulkeepers. We're helpless against them. It made me see that he was as scared as I am. We both have to trust that God will look out for us."

"All of us have to trust in that, Malini. But why do you say you're not a Soulkeeper? Did Dr. Silva tell you she was wrong?"

"No, but it's obvious. I was completely helpless against that Watcher today, Jacob." Her eyes swam as she said it. "I'm lucky to be alive."

"It was a bad situation. I know why you did it, but I wish you'd stayed on the other side of the fence."

Malini became intensely interested in the corner of her comforter.

"And, if you need someone to talk to, talk to me. I'm your boyfriend. I want to be who you come to."

Malini's mouth opened on an intake of breath. "You're jealous," she stated firmly.

"No," Jacob retorted. "I simply want to be there for you."

"Bullshit. You don't want me to talk to Dane because you think he wants me ... a little."

"Should I be worried, Malini? Do you want Dane, even a little?"

"Do you want Mara, even a little?"

"Mara? When did this become about Mara?"

"Since you couldn't take your eyes off of her from the moment she walked through that portal."

Jacob shook has head and scoffed in her direction. "Not true. And this conversation is so not what I had in mind when I came over here tonight."

"Hmmphf," Malini replied. Her arms had worked their way across her stomach.

He reached out and drew her into his chest, separating her hands in the process and wrapping them around his neck. "I love you, Malini. Only you."

Eventually her chocolate-brown eyes softened. His lips found hers and she welcomed his kiss, eager for more. Lowering her head to her pillow, he stretched out over her.

"What *did* you have in mind, Jacob?" she asked.

"I'm not exactly sure but this is more like it," he said into her mouth.

She reached up for his face and it was a long time before they said anything else.

* * * * *

At dawn, Jacob returned to the Laudners', feeling a pang of guilt that he'd spent the night at Malini's without permission. Nothing had happened except for some serious making out. They'd decided last year that they weren't ready for anything more. He'd simply wanted to stay to protect her and ended up falling asleep with her cuddled against his chest.

He scaled the rose lattice. Pushing open the window, he slid in carefully. It took a minute for his eyes to adjust to the dim room. The first thing he noticed was that his door was cracked open. Had he locked it after all? The second thing he noticed, as his line of sight passed over the bed, was the handle of a large knife protruding from the Jacob-styled pillow decoy.

The blade was positioned exactly where his heart should have been.

Chapter 7
Investigation

It was his mother's idea to call in Dr. Silva and Mara. Once Jacob had crept down to her makeshift bed on the Laudners' couch and told her about the stabbing, she'd texted the news to Dr. Silva. The next second, he was holding hands with Mara in the living room. They'd ascended the stairs hand in hand to the place where Jacob would be dead if he hadn't been at Malini's.

As Soulkeeper powers went, Mara's had to be the most mind blowing. The only thing keeping Jacob animated were her fingers linked with his. He couldn't stop looking at the bird outside his window. It was frozen mid-flight, suspended open-winged in midair. Everything was paused. Everything but the four of them who were connected to Mara by linked fingers.

"Remember, if you break contact with me, you'll stop like everything else," Mara said.

"Jacob, I'm happy to see you are not the one under the knife, but where the hell were you last night?" Lillian asked. Her voice had changed from a Soulkeeper's to a mother's and Jacob blushed as every eye in the room fell on him for an answer.

"I was with Malini."

"All night?" Lillian snapped.

"Yes. I was worried about her after what happened yesterday. I wanted to make sure she was okay."

"And you needed all night to do that?"

"Considering there's someone in Paris trying to stab us in our sleep, I'd say, 'yes.'"

Dr. Silva interrupted. "Perhaps it would be beneficial if we focused on the task at hand. Jacob, was the window unlocked the entire night?"

"Yeah. I went out the window, so it was unlocked."

"So, it could've been someone from the outside."

Dr. Silva waved her hand and a purple light shone on the handle of the knife. "No prints."

Jacob shook his head. "The door to my room was open when I came home. I'd locked it before I left."

"Are you certain?"

"Yes."

"It's Katrina," Lillian said.

Dr. Silva turned a quizzical eye toward Lillian.

"We think she's under a Watcher's influence. She's been acting strangely since the moment she came home. I can't figure out how it's getting to her though. To make her do something like this, it would have to be feeding her large quantities of elixir."

"I agree," Dr. Silva said. "If it was Katrina, a Watcher must be very close."

"If it is her, what do we do?" Mara asked. "We can't take her out and if we get the police involved it could be a disaster. We don't need a bunch of people snooping around right now. Our cover is more important than ever."

"Plus, if we incapacitate Katrina, we'll never find the Watcher. We need to use her to lead us to it," Dr. Silva said.

"This is my niece we're talking about," Lillian said. "She's no sweetheart but she's also not a killer. I couldn't stomach the pain it would cause John and Carolyn if anything happened to her."

"Once the Watcher is dead, Lillian, Katrina will return to normal as soon as the elixir wears off. Dane Michaels was influenced last year and he lost the drive to hurt Jacob almost immediately once Auriel couldn't reach him anymore."

"How do we know a Watcher didn't come through the window, stab Jacob's bed, and then open the door to search the house when he realized it wasn't him?" Mara asked.

"Well, I'm still alive, so it didn't reach me," Lillian said.

"Maybe it didn't know what you are," Dr. Silva said.

"Maybe it was scared away by something else," Mara added.

Dr. Silva tilted her head. "Good point. Let's pay Katrina a visit and see if there are any clues to how the Watcher is influencing her. For the Watcher to be effective there has to be a source, something to maintain its influence over her when it returns to Nod. Look for an elixir or pills."

Hand in hand they walked to Katrina's room and slipped inside her door. She was curled under the covers, frozen in a state of peaceful sleep. Dr. Silva scanned the room.

"I can smell Watcher here. It's strong. It's very possible it just left, but I don't see any obvious signs of what it was doing in here."

With a flick of Dr. Silva's hand the drawers pulled out, the closet opened, and the bed-skirt flipped up.

"Shit, she folds her socks!" Mara said.

"Yeah, Katrina is a total neat freak," Jacob added.

"There are worse habits to have," Lillian added.

"There's nothing here," said Dr. Silva. "I don't see anything that could hold an elixir."

She waved her hand and the room righted itself.

"So, do you think it was Katrina who tried to stab me? Or was it the Watcher?"

"I'm not sure, Jacob. But I think we must all be very careful from this moment forward. There's a Watcher in our midst and it knows who you are. If it was your cousin who stabbed those blankets, she might try to finish the job," Dr. Silva said. "How long is she here?"

"The entire week. She's on spring break. But Malini and I go back to school Monday."

"Good. Try not to be alone with Katrina. And, Lillian, I would keep that bed on the couch if I were you."

"And sleep with one eye open…" Lillian said, nodding.

"What about Jacob?" Mara said. "Are we going to do anything about keeping him from becoming a shish kabob over the next six nights?"

"I'll stay with Malini," Jacob said.

"Not a good idea, Jacob," his mom said. "Besides the fact that I'm completely uncomfortable with you spending the night with your girlfriend at sixteen, have you stopped to think what would happen if you got caught? Jim Gupta grounded her for six months for what happened in October. You may never be allowed to see her again. This isn't just about you. Jim could make it twice as hard for us to work with her in the future."

"She needs protection."

"I don't know if that should be you, Jacob," Dr. Silva said. "Wherever this Watcher is, he's targeted you. You wouldn't want to lure the Watcher to her. I agree she needs protection. Gideon and I will keep watch around her house at night. But I agree with Lillian. It's not in anyone's best interest for you to stay the night with Malini."

"Fine, so where do I go?" Jacob asked.

"You can stay with me at Dr. Silva's," Mara said. "It makes sense. We can protect each other. Maybe Lillian should come, too."

"Mara is right. My house is enchanted against Watchers. It's the safest place and there's plenty of room."

"The Laudners will notice if I'm gone," Lillian said. "All it would take is Carolyn getting up in the middle of the night for a drink of water to notice me missing. I would never hear the end of it."

"I'll build you an illusion, Lillian, but I do think you should stay with me. The one thing we've learned from all of this is that what we heard in Chicago was no empty threat. There is a Watcher here, among us, and we have to assume it knows who we are. Whoever plunged that knife into Jacob's bed knows he's not dead. The fact that it left the knife in the pillow is a warning. It wants us to know it was here. I have a feeling, the next time it tries to kill one of us, it won't give up so easily."

The room grew quiet as each of them processed the truth in Dr. Silva's words. Jacob looked at his mom and saw her eyes had gone glossy with tears. A chill ran up his spine. None of them were safe. Evil had come to Paris.

"We've got to go," Mara rasped. "I can't hold it much longer." Her face had gone ashen white and Jacob noticed her hand was icy cold within his. Her lips were turning blue.

Lillian led the way. Dr. Silva closed the door to Katrina's room behind them. Once they were safely inside Jacob's room, Mara dropped Dr. Silva's hand and rang the bell she'd stored in her pocket. The frozen bird in Jacob's window continued on its way as if nothing had happened. Mara released Jacob's fingers and fell into the orange chair by the window.

"That's a really powerful gift," Jacob whispered to Mara.

Flushed from the return of her body heat, she smiled. "Thank you."

Dr. Silva pulled the knife from Jacob's decoy and tucked it under her arm. Circling one hand over the other, she conjured a purple flame and tossed it at his bed. His bedspread stitched itself up and loose stuffing tucked itself back into his pillow. By the time the purple magic had burnt itself out, his bed looked like new.

"Thanks!" Jacob said.

"You are welcome." Dr. Silva paused, tilting her head. "I believe the heavy footfalls I'm hearing mean John and Carolyn are awake. Mara, let's make use of Jacob's window."

Jacob didn't hear anything, but he knew better than to question Dr. Silva. She raised the glass panel and leapt through, floating to the ground without the aid of the rose lattice. Mara sighed and climbed down the much more human way. Jacob waved as they crossed the yard toward Dr. Silva's gothic Victorian.

He turned back toward his mom, who waited just inside the door.

"Do we need to talk about what happened with Malini last night?" Lillian whispered.

"I told you what happened," Jacob said.

Lillian rested her hands on his shoulders and looked him in the eye. "Tell me the truth. Did you have sex with her?"

"No, I didn't. I swear."

"You know you can tell me anything, Jacob, but you need to be honest with me. Did you have sex with her?"

"I am being honest. No."

His mom relaxed slightly, the tension bleeding from her shoulders. She embraced him in a firm hug. "I knew you were smarter than that, but I needed to be sure." She drifted toward the door and crept into the hall.

Jacob fell onto his newly repaired bed, thinking about Katrina, the Watcher, and the Soulkeeper he'd just seen stop time. He wondered if he'd ever have a normal day again. And more than anything, he dreaded having to explain it all to Malini.

Chapter 8
Family

Malini held the phone to her ear, hoping she'd put enough space between her and her father to be discreet. He wouldn't be happy if he knew she was talking to Jacob.

"I need to talk to you, Malini. Can you come into the shop?" Jacob's voice broke and Malini couldn't tell if it was the reception on her cell phone or something more.

"Your voice sounds funny. Is everything okay?"

"I'd rather talk to you in person."

"If you can't tell me over the phone, it will have to wait. We're in Springfield for the day."

"Springfield?"

Malini cupped her hand over her mouth and whispered into the phone. "Yeah, I totally forgot my dad's birthday. We're at the Abraham Lincoln Presidential Museum. You know my dad."

There was a long pause on the other end of the connection.

"Jacob, are you there?"

"Yeah. When do you think you'll be back?"

"Late. We're having dinner here and then it's over two hours home. Can it wait until tomorrow at school?"

Jacob sighed.

Malini's father tapped her on the shoulder. "Who is that on the phone, Malini?" he said. "You'll miss the log cabin."

"It's Dane, Dad," Malini lied.

"Nice. Dane's okay but I'm not?" Jacob groused.

Malini didn't know what to say.

"Sounds like you've got to go. Don't worry about anything, Malini. I'll talk to you tomorrow."

"Okay. See you tomorrow."

She touched the end call button.

"Look, Malini. He taught himself how to read," her dad said excitedly, motioning for her to come over. There was a model of Abe as a teen outside the log cabin. The wax figure held a book in his hand.

"That can't be true, Dad. Who teaches themselves how to read?"

"Abe Lincoln, that's who."

Malini followed her parents through the one-room cabin, wondering how much was real and how much was legend.

"Dad, what is with your obsession with Abraham Lincoln anyway? Why not ... I don't know ... Gandhi?"

"What? Because we are Indian, I should have an Indian hero?"

"I didn't mean it that way. It just seems sort of random."

"Come, Malini. I want to show you something." Her father hooked his arm inside her elbow. Her mother, who had been staring fixedly at the pot over the fake fire, accepted his other arm.

They exited the cabin and made their way down the next hall. Her father stopped them in front of a photograph of a black man whose back was ripped to shreds. Malini had to turn away.

"That's awful," she said.

"There's more."

He led her to a scene titled *The Slave Auction.* The depiction of a family being torn apart by slave traders broke her heart. She had to remind herself that the models weren't real.

"This is so depressing, Dad."

"Wait, one more thing."

He led her through a room of caricatures criticizing Lincoln. "Did you know so many people hated him while he was alive?" Malini asked. "These are some of the worst political cartoons I've ever seen."

"Oh he wasn't always a popular president, Malini."

He stopped in a room called *A Soldier's Story* and took a seat on a wooden bench. He patted the wood next to him. She sat down between her parents. A movie began called *The Civil War in Four Minutes*. Malini watched as the first shots of the war progressed into a massacre that divided the country. In the end, over a million casualties were tallied between north and south.

"Wow," she said. "I had no idea so many people died."

Her father placed his hand on her leg. "Abraham Lincoln is my hero because somehow he knew that this was the right thing to do. Somehow he knew that this was all worth it."

"It is incredible. He must have questioned what he was doing plenty of times. He certainly didn't seem to have much support."

Her father stood up, nodding, and proceeded toward the exit. Malini followed until her mother nudged her elbow and purposefully slowed to put distance between them and her father.

"What your father will never tell you is that it is personal," she said. Her mother's long brown braid fell forward on her shoulder as she leaned in toward Malini.

"What do you mean?"

"I was not of your father's caste in India. We should have never been allowed to marry. We were barely older than you are now when we fell in love. The reason he loves it here is that my class is not an issue. And he thanks that man for the favor." She pointed at a wax model of Abraham Lincoln.

"I never knew. How did dad convince Grandma and Grandpa to let him marry you?"

"He didn't. We eloped. It wasn't until *you* were born that they came around again."

Malini couldn't believe it. Her grandparents had always been supportive and loving. She couldn't picture her grandfather being so closed-minded.

They'd reached a room that depicted the death of Lincoln's son, Willie. Malini followed the crowd forward, lost in thought.

"So the reason he moved us to America ... the reason he's so in love with this country ... is because of you? Because here, everyone is equal?"

"Yes. Did you know our first house had a dirt floor?"

"No, I didn't."

"Your father has done well for us." She smiled.

Malini tossed her arms around her mother's neck and squeezed her tight. "Thank you for telling me."

At the edge of the crowd, they paused in an alcove called *The Hall of Sorrows.* A wax figure of Mary Todd Lincoln was posed, weeping near a dark window.

"She was crazy, you know? Had to be committed to a mental institution near the end of her life. She wore only black after Lincoln was assassinated," her mother said.

Malini frowned at the grieving statue. The billowy layers of black lace on the dress must have weighed a ton. How itchy the high-necked collar must have been. But it was the red stone broach pinned at Mary Todd Lincoln's throat that drew Malini's eye again and again.

* * * * *

Jacob watched the clock tick, willing the hands to move faster. Thankfully, Laudner's Flowers and Gifts closed at five on Sundays. He didn't think he could take another hour on his feet.

"Go ahead and flip the sign, Jacob. There's only five minutes left. I'm sure it will be okay," Lillian said. They'd arranged to work the entire day for John and Carolyn. It was an ample justification for staying away from Katrina. Coupled with a mother/son dinner date, they'd effectively excused themselves until bedtime.

Jacob reached for the heavy cardboard *open* sign and was about to flip it over when a large woman with curly red hair appeared in front of the glass door. Her arms were occupied with an oversized crate of potted tulips and she was crying. Jacob recognized Fran Westcott even through the smudged mascara that made her look like a raccoon. He dropped the sign and pushed open the door for her.

"Thank you, Jacob," she said as she stepped into the shop.

Lillian lifted the box from Fran's arms. "What can we do for you, Fran? It looks like you're having a rough day."

"I know this isn't right. There's nothing wrong with the flowers, Lillian, and I know it's against your policy to return them at this point. But I can't look at them. I can't." Fran began weeping again.

Lillian set the box down and wrapped her arm around the woman's ample shoulders. "Fran, don't be silly. Given the circumstances, of course we'll take them back. I'm so sorry you're going through this. Has there been any word at all about Stephanie?"

"No. Nothing." Fran mopped her face with a tissue from the little purse that hung from her elbow. "She was at a party the night before. Her roommate says there was a boy. She left for home with a boy she'd never met before and she hasn't been seen since. And do you know, no one had ever seen that boy before. As far as we know, he didn't even go to UI."

"Did her roommate know his name?"

"No. Sickening, isn't it? My daughter spent the night with a boy she'd never met before and her roommate didn't even know his name. What was she thinking?" A new wave of weeping overcame her. "Atrocious behavior! I shouldn't be telling you at all. As if this town needs something else to gossip about."

"Fran, Jacob and I aren't going to tell anyone about that," Lillian said. She shot a glance at Jacob.

"Of course not. Mrs. Westcott, sometimes people do things they regret later. Everyone deserves a second chance. I'm not going to say a word."

"The thing is, I just keep hoping she's still with him. Maybe this whole thing is just irresponsible behavior and she'll show up on my door with this boy. Oh how I hope I'll see the day when all I've got to worry about is a bunch of rumors. Oh hell!" Her tissue was soaked. Lillian grabbed a new one from behind the counter and placed it in her hand.

After several minutes, Mrs. Westcott seemed to pull herself together.

"How about that refund?" Lillian asked.

Mrs. Westcott nodded and followed Lillian to the cash register. With cash in hand, she didn't linger. "You Laudners are good people. Always have been."

Jacob flipped the sign and locked the door behind her.

Chapter 9
Safe House

Jacob remembered the first time he'd seen this room. He'd been searching for Dr. Silva's notebook. That day seemed like an eternity ago.

The furniture was still covered with white sheets, except for the bed. Dr. Silva had uncovered it before he settled in for the night. Only, he wasn't settled. Every time he closed his eyes he saw black scaly skin. Every dream he had was a nightmare.

After hours of tossing and turning, he gave up and quietly descended the stairs to the kitchen. He poured himself a glass of water and sat down at the table.

"Milk works better, you know?" Mara said from the hallway. "Warm milk. That's what they say anyway. Personally, I can't stomach the taste, but if you're desperate."

"What are you doing up?" Jacob asked.

"I could ask you the same thing."

"Couldn't sleep. I guess I dozed a couple of times but I keep having nightmares. The kind where something's chasing you."

"Me, too. I know this place is enchanted but I don't feel safe." Mara placed her hands on the back of a chair at the table as if she couldn't decide whether to sit down or not.

"I feel safe, I just think there's something more I should be doing."

"You mean like protecting your girlfriend yourself?" Mara asked.

"Yeah, exactly like that," Jacob answered.

"Gideon will do a good job. He won't let anything happen to her."

"I know, but it should be me, and I feel rotten that she doesn't know what's going on."

"Why didn't you tell her?"

"She was gone all day. I didn't have a chance."

"You've never heard of a phone?"

"I called her, okay, but explaining that Watchers tried to kill me and might be after her too didn't seem like the best conversation to have over a cell phone. That's more of an in-person thing, don't you think?"

"You're probably right." Mara pulled out the chair and sat down. For the first time, he noticed her pajamas.

"Nice PJs. You been a fan of SpongeBob a long time?"

"Practically since birth. But to tell you the truth, I have these because they remind me of the day I became a Soulkeeper."

Jacob took a sip of water and made the gimme sign with his hand. "There's more to that story."

She frowned. "I usually don't talk about it."

"Well we could sit here in silence or you could share."

She leaned back into her chair. "I was twelve when I became a Soulkeeper. My mother was beating up my father."

Jacob raised his eyebrows.

"I saw that. See, this isn't a happy story. That's why I don't tell people."

"Have you ever told anyone?"

"Just my Helper. Until recently, he was the only Soulkeeper I knew."

"Tell me," Jacob said. He leaned toward her and placed a hand on top of hers. "I promise, I won't judge."

Mara stared at his hand until he felt self-conscious and pulled it back to his side of the table. She continued with her story.

"People always think it's the other way around, that because the guy is bigger and stronger, he's always the beater. But my mom was a boozer and when she got violent my dad didn't want to hurt her, so he took it. I mean like, he took a beating regularly, every time she'd get drunk, which was practically always. Looking back, it was really bad but, you have to understand, at the time I was used to it. It was a regular thing.

"Well, this one time when I was twelve, my mom got really drunk and decided fists weren't good enough. She reached for a kitchen knife, the big one in the block. I guess it's called a chef's knife. I was sitting in the living room watching SpongeBob, trying not to think about the sound of them fighting behind me, when everything went quiet. I knew something was wrong because they were never quiet. Mom was a loud drunk. I turned around and saw she had the knife aimed at my father's chest. He had his hands up like he'd surrendered and she was smiling like it was all a big joke. And then she dove for him."

Jacob tried his best to keep his expression neutral, but inside he couldn't believe what he was hearing. He gave a small nod to let her know he was listening.

"There was this bell we kept on our coffee table, some antique piece of crap my mom had picked up at a garage sale. It was heavy and it was metal. I grabbed it and leapt over the couch. I wanted to use it to block the knife. But when it rang, everything stopped. I didn't know what the hell was going on. I don't know how long I stood there watching a freeze frame of my mother trying to kill my father. But at some point I turned my mother's wrist so that the knife pointed away from my father's chest.

"Finally, it occurred to me to ring the bell again. When I did, I realized that when I turned the knife away from my father, I'd pointed the blade toward my mother's chest. When time started again, she couldn't stop her momentum. She plunged that chef's knife into her own chest. I watched my mother stab herself with SpongeBob playing in the background."

"Oh my God, Mara. That's…"

"Horrible. Awful. Tragic. Excruciatingly painful." The words dripped with regret.

Jacob shook his head. "It wasn't your fault. The day I became a Soulkeeper, I almost killed two boys in my class. The water threw them thirty feet into a wall. All it would have taken was something sharp or the wrong angle and they'd be dead."

"Huh. Well, my mom didn't die, but see when the cops came and I tried to explain what had happened, it sounded crazy. I didn't know what I was, so I told the truth. Then I told the truth again and again to a bunch of different people. And before you know it, I was committed to the Jacksonville psychiatric hospital."

Jacob buried his fingers in his hair. Suddenly, his head felt like it weighed a million pounds. "How did your Helper find you?"

"He didn't for a full year. I lived there for three hundred and sixty seven days. And you know what? My parents never came to visit me. No one came to visit me. Then one day, an old man asked to see me. Right there in the visitor's center he explained to me what I was. His name was Dean Bell. Ironic huh. I had a Helper named Mr. Bell."

"How did he get you out?"

"Oh, he just handed me a bell, held my hand, and told me to use it. I lived three years with him. A Watcher killed him during a mission last year. It was just the two of us. We killed it first but ... I couldn't save him. That's when I moved to Chicago."

"What about your parents? Didn't they come looking for you?"

"I don't even think they noticed I was gone."

"Mara, I'm glad you told me but there's something I've gotta know."

"What?"

"Why in the world would you want to remember that? I mean, the SpongeBob pajamas part."

"Because it taught me the power of my gift. I can stop time, Jacob. If I wanted to, I could walk into a bank and take all the money out of the open drawers. I could move someone I didn't like in front of a bus. I wear the SpongeBob pajamas so that I remember how it felt to watch someone I thought I wanted dead plunge a knife into her chest. I didn't like it, Jacob. SpongeBob reminds me to live by the rules even though I don't have to."

She brushed the hot pink streak of her bangs back from her eyes. For a moment, Jacob was speechless, mulling over Mara's profound history. When it was clear the silence was making her uncomfortable, he searched for something to say.

"You could've just kept the kitchen knife."

Mara squinted her eyes in his direction. "What?"

"Instead of buying the pajamas, you could've bought a kitchen knife."

"Do you have a problem with the pineapple under the sea, Lau."

"In fact I do. I think it's like crack for third graders."

"Nice."

In the quiet that followed, they both tried to squelch a wave of giggles. "You called SpongeBob crack," Mara said, laughing.

Jacob stood. "Well, I'm going to try to get some sleep."

"Okay. See you in the morning," she said. "Oh, and Jacob?"

"Yeah."

"I'm sure everything will be all right with Malini. She'll understand."

"I hope you're right."

He climbed the staircase, hoping he could be a friend to Mara. After all she'd been through, she needed one.

Chapter 10
Planning Committee

Malini tossed her orange tray down across from Jacob and Dane. At some point during the school year, they'd migrated to Dane's table with Amy Barger and Phillip Westcott. When Amy broke up with Dane, she defected to Jacob and Malini's old table with her girlfriends. Phillip, who had never fully accepted the Dane-Jacob friendship, remained at the table but he and Mike perched on the end with a full two-person gap between his section and theirs. It was pretty clear that there was still a line in the sand. Dane was just on the other side of it.

"Good news, Jacob. I think my dad is ready to un-ground me. At breakfast, I mentioned studying together this week and he didn't freak out," Malini said.

"So, he said, 'Yes?'"

"Not exactly. He sort of tilted his head to the side. But it wasn't a no." She grinned, taking a bite of her salad.

"How was Springfield?"

"Good actually. My dad and I hardly fought at all."

"Cool."

"By the way, thank you for coming by Saturday night."

"You're welcome," Dane and Jacob said together.

Malini looked back and forth between the two of them. "I meant Jacob, Dane."

"Oh," Dane said. "Sorry … I thought, because I was there and you were still grounded…"

"I came by anyway," Jacob said curtly. "Later." He gave Dane some seriously hostile eye contact.

"Will you guys chill? Please?" Malini asked. "Can you come by again tonight, Jake?" Malini asked.

"I don't think I can," Jacob said. "Something happened Saturday night. Something I need to tell you about."

Malini leaned forward just as Dane did until she realized Phillip had stopped eating and was watching them suspiciously.

"Maybe there's a better place for this conversation," Malini whispered, tilting her head in Phillip's direction.

Jacob became interested in his meatloaf. Dane shifted in his seat. The instant quiet was as suspicious as the huddling had been. Thankfully, Dane came up with alternative conversation.

"Have you guys thought about prom?" he asked, louder than necessary.

"Do we need to think about it now? It isn't until May, right?" Malini said, rolling her eyes. Jacob glared at her. It was a sore subject.

"True, but it's the end of March. They're starting the planning committee. I thought we could all, you know, work on it together."

Jacob pressed a finger to his lips and squinted at Dane incredulously. *"You* want to join the prom committee?"

Thinking it was a joke, Malini burst out laughing, but stopped when she noticed the look on Dane's face.

He lowered his voice again, a blush forming on his cheeks. "Since I broke up with Amy, there's no one to go with. The committee would be an excuse for me to be there alone. You know, you guys have each other but I'm kind of on my own here."

"Don't be ridiculous," Malini said. "You're the most popular boy in our class."

Dane swallowed a gulp of his lemonade. "Not anymore."

Jacob and Malini exchanged looks. It was true. Befriending them had cost him his reputation.

"Prom committee sounds fun," Malini said. When Jacob didn't say anything, she kicked him under the table.

A grin stretched across Jacob's face. "Prom committee? I was planning on joining before you asked."

Dane snickered. "Thanks, you two. The first meeting is Thursday."

Jacob reached for Malini's hand. "Speaking of meetings, McNaulty's after school? I have to talk to you."

"Sure, but it will have to wait until four. I'm working in the lab for Mrs. Jacques."

"My God, Malini. How many jobs do you have?"

"Counting my fake job with Dr. Silva and the part-time position with your uncle, three. My dad is loving it."

"Damn. Guess who's paying for prom tickets?" Jacob said.

Malini kicked him again beneath the table.

"Ow! That one really hurt."

"So, am I invited to this super secret meeting?" Dane asked.

Jacob stuffed his mouth full of meatloaf. It was obvious he was avoiding the question. Malini felt obligated to answer. Dane was part of this whether Jacob wanted to admit it or not, and he had every right to know. "Yes, Dane. I'm sure if Jacob has anything to tell me, he needs to tell you, too. You're as much a part of this as I am."

The look Jacob shot her told her he didn't agree, but he didn't say anything to the contrary.

"Cool. I'll see you there."

Dane grinned like he'd just won some huge contest. Malini wondered if he realized the only prize when it came to dealing with Watchers was surviving.

Chapter 11
Anatomy & Physiology

"What are we doing today?" Malini asked Mrs. Jacques. The science lab was deserted and her voice seemed unnaturally loud in the empty room.

"First things first, I need you to clean off the lab tables. Anything that looks valuable, you can put in the lost and found basket by the window. Otherwise, throw everything away and wipe down the tables with this disinfectant."

Malini wedged a roll of paper towels under her arm and picked up the bottle of blue liquid.

"When you're done with that," Mrs. Jacques continued, "place one dissection kit at each pair of seats." She opened the top of a large cardboard box that sat on her desk and started pulling out items. "There are three things in here: the tray, the instruments, and the frogs. Please cut open the instruments but leave them in the bag so none of the pins get lost. Don't cut open the frogs or the entire room will smell like formalin."

A wave of nausea rushed over Malini. Her face must have paled because Mrs. Jacques snorted. "Are you okay? Don't worry. They're not gross or anything. In fact, this company preserves them so well, they almost look alive." She pulled a shrink-wrapped frog from the box. It did look alive but for some reason this was not a comfort to Malini.

"I can do it," Malini forced herself to say. In her head, she was planning to use the chemistry tongs to carry the frogs by the corner of their packaging. No way was she touching those things.

"Good, because you'll be dissecting one in Anatomy and Physiology tomorrow. Might as well get comfortable with the idea." Mrs. Jacques flashed a sardonic smile as if she found her student's discomfort with dissection both ridiculous and amusing.

Malini responded by heading to the first table and clearing it of the used paper towels, pencils, and scratch paper that had been left behind. She tossed everything in the garbage before spraying and wiping down the table.

"Looks like you've got it under control. I'll be grading papers in the teacher's lounge if you need me." She picked up her stack of work and shouldered her way out the door. It swung shut behind her.

"Right," Malini said, finally free of Mrs. Jacques' watchful eye. "Sure, I'll handle your dead frogs for you. Why, I love the feel of plastic-wrapped amphibian in the afternoon." She rolled her eyes toward the door.

She made short work of the cleanup. Then she doled out the trays and instruments as instructed. The frogs she left for last. Using chemistry tongs, she lifted each one out of the box by the plastic corner, flipping them onto the dissection trays one by one. Unfortunately, the plastic was slippery enough that it became like a game, trying to get the frogs into the trays before the weight of the animal slipped her grip. She was fine for the first several tables but on the last one, farthest from the box, the specimen slipped and landed in a rubbery splat on the tile floor. Sighing, she abandoned the tongs and decided to put her big girl panties on. She picked it up with her hands.

She was surprised how fake it felt resting in her palm, the plastic wrap a barrier against the dead thing underneath. It was sad, really. In the wild, when a thing died, it decayed and became food for other living things. The great circle of life. This was permanently dead—preserved in a state that should have been transitional. She wasn't sure why it bothered her now. She'd dissected things before and understood the importance. There wouldn't be doctors without dissection. But for some reason this particular frog made her stomach sink.

Her palm tingled. Maybe her hand was falling asleep? Malini tried to dump the frog onto the last tray but the plastic wrap stuck to her skin. She gave it a shake. Sweat beaded around the plastic. She shook her hand again, harder. The frog didn't fall to the table. The tingle advanced to a burning sensation. At first it was minor, like a sunburn, but soon it felt like someone was holding her hand to a hot skillet. Her skin was on fire.

She tugged franticly at the plastic. It didn't come easily. A patch of skin from the heel of her hand ripped away. Blisters formed near the edge of the packaging. The plastic bubbled against her palm. The chemicals used to preserve the frog must have somehow leached out of the bag!

Bolting toward the sink, she cranked the water and flushed her hand. She screamed as the spray hit her injured skin. Hot and cold comingled painfully in her palm and the plastic oozed from her hand, taking a layer of skin with it. Red and blistered, black burnt-looking skin edged the wound. The cold water helped. The burning pain turned into a dull ache, just as Mrs. Jacques burst through the science room door.

"I heard a scream! Malini, are you all right?" she asked.

"I ... I..." Malini began over her shoulder, but as she looked down into the basin she couldn't finish her sentence. For one, her hand was completely healed and ... and... "The frog is alive!"

Mrs. Jacques ran to her side, shutting off the water and rubbing Malini's back. "It's okay, Malini. Take a deep breath." The teacher inhaled sharply. Next to a mangled piece of plastic the grass green frog leapt repeatedly into the shiny stainless steel wall of the sink, not only alive but vigorous.

"Oh my God. I have never seen such a thing in my twenty years of teaching. That company is going to hear from me!" She handed Malini a paper towel. "I know it's upsetting, dear. To think they've packaged an animal alive. It's horrific. I can't believe the poor thing survived."

Malini's eyes turned toward the other frogs, the ones on the trays. She searched for any sign of movement, anything to help her believe the frog had been alive in the package the whole time.

"Don't worry, honey. I'll check the rest of them. Hopefully it's an isolated incident. You'd better go home. You look woozy. Do you want me to call your father to come pick you up?"

Malini shook her head. "No, I'm fine, Mrs. Jacques," she forced herself to say. "But I think I will go, if it's okay with you."

"Of course."

Malini backed through the door, twisting the paper towel between her fingers. Alone in the hallway, she looked down at her palm, pain-free beneath the paper. Her skin was its usual shade, perfectly healed.

"Shit, this is not ... right," she said under her breath and bolted out the door. She had to find Jacob and talk to Dr. Silva. This wasn't normal. It definitely wasn't natural. But Malini was afraid to even consider what it might mean.

Chapter 12
McNaulty's

Malini entered McNaulty's all but running to her usual booth. She came up behind Jacob just as he was finishing a sentence. She didn't hear what he had said but his voice was raised and Dane's jaw was clenched.

"What's going on here?" Malini slid in next to Jacob.

Dane answered, "I asked Jacob if he'd like for me to take you to the prom, I mean, if your dad didn't allow *him* to take you. He wasn't keen on the idea."

"Hell no, I'm not *keen* on it," Jacob said.

Malini held up her hand. "Stop! First of all, this conversation is just stupid. It's much too early to be worrying about prom. Second, something's happened that's much more important!" Malini thrust her hand out palm up between them.

There was a pause as the boys looked at her hand.

"What? What is it, Malini?" Jacob whispered. He slid his hand into hers.

"My … my hand was burnt and now it's not … and there was a frog. I'm sure it was dead and now it's alive. There's something wrong with me or maybe this is it. Maybe this is how I'm a Soulkeeper."

"Slow down, Malini," Dane said. "Tell us what happened."

"I was in the lab. I was holding a dead frog, one of the shrink-wrapped ones Mrs. Jacques buys for dissection. My hand started to burn and the plastic wrap melted and then the frog jumped away. My hand was burnt, red and black and covered with blisters. Look, it's healed." She let go of Jacob's hand and thrust it out again. "What do you think it means?"

Jacob ran his hand through his hair and exchanged glances with Dane.

"Maybe her power is fire?" Dane whispered. "Like maybe you guys balance each other. You're water and she's fire. Sharkboy and Lavagirl." He laughed.

"It's not funny, Dane," Malini said.

"Gideon did say we were drawn together, spirit to spirit. Maybe that's what he was sensing, that our powers would balance each other," Jacob said.

"But what about the frog?" Malini asked.

"Are you sure it was really dead? Maybe it was just like hibernating and when you melted the plastic it got a good breath of air and revived," Dane said.

"I guess." Malini shrugged.

Jacob rubbed her hand between his own. "The only other explanation is that you raised the dead." He gave a breathy chuckle as he said it but a chill ran up her spine.

"Don't say that, Jacob. It's wrong. No one can raise the dead."

"What if you're a Healer?" Jacob asked. The word rolled out of his mouth like a multi-legged alien life form that the two of them wanted to pretend wasn't wriggling on the table between their cokes.

"Is that a bad thing?" Dane asked. "Healer sounds like a good thing."

Malini shook her head. "Healers are very rare, Dane. There can only be one or two on the Earth at any one time. Plus, Dr. Silva tested me for that. One of our first meetings, she sliced my shoulder with a kitchen knife. It bled like you wouldn't believe. She said it ruled out my being a Healer."

"Yeah. She tried something similar with me." Jacob lowered his hand from his head and pressed his palm into the table. "You need to talk to Dr. Silva. She'll be able to tell you what this means."

"Until then, avoid dead frogs," Dane said.

Jacob grinned.

"You guys, you're acting like this is no big deal!" she said.

Jacob's face turned serious. "It is a big deal. But we've always known you were a Soulkeeper. And now *you* know. You may not fully understand what your gift is, but at least you know for sure that you've got one."

Dane folded his arms over his chest and leaned back in his seat. "One more person to protect me."

The look on his face broke Malini's heart. She knew that look, that vulnerability. Even with what happened, she felt it, too. Like their destiny was not their own since the day they'd learned about the Watchers. She felt like a pawn in some massive chess game and she didn't even know what piece she was yet.

She reached across the table and laid her hand on Dane's arm. "You can take care of yourself, Dane. You may not be a Soulkeeper, but you are one tough dude and you make up the difference in heart."

It was Jacob's turn to roll his eyes and stare out the window. But Dane was quick to show he appreciated the sentiment. "Thanks, *Malini*. I needed to hear that."

His voice held a twinge of belligerence, a tangle of things unsaid that left all of them silent and looking in opposite directions.

Malini attempted to rescue the conversation. "So, what's this big news you were trying to tell me at lunch, anyway?"

Jacob leaned into the table, bracing himself on his elbows and looking from side to side. Malini and Dane checked over their shoulders and leaned in as well.

"There's a Watcher in Paris again," Jacob said.

Dane paled. "Who? Where?"

"We don't know but we think it's influenced Katrina. When I came home yesterday there was a knife sunk into my bed."

Malini's hand went to her heart. "What?"

"She's been acting really odd. We don't actually know if she wielded the knife but Dr. Silva sensed Watcher all over her. It's definitely close."

"Dr. Silva came over? What about the Laudners?"

"She had Mara stop time so that we could investigate."

"You mean, so that Mara could investigate—"

"No, we held hands and everything else stopped but us."

Malini squelched a tide of jealousy that rose from the pit of her stomach. Dr. Silva and Lillian were undoubtedly part of the handholding. She was sure it wasn't romantic. "So, what did you find?"

"We couldn't tell for sure if Katrina tried to kill me or if it was the Watcher. All we know is that a Watcher has come to Paris, Katrina is influenced, and they've targeted me."

Malini swallowed hard. "What did Dr. Silva say we should do about that?"

"We're going to wait and watch Katrina. Eventually she'll have to lead us to it."

"You'll have to stay with me then. We can't have her stabbing you in your sleep," Malini said.

"The Watchers know who I am, Malini. The fact that they tried to stab me means it's me they're after. I can't lead them to you."

Malini squeezed Jacob's hand and turned in the booth to face him full on. "That's a chance I'm willing to take."

He pulled away from her, pressing his back against the window. "It's not one I'm willing to take. I was the one who killed Mordechai. I'm the one they want. They don't know who you are, Malini, and we intend to keep it that way."

"We?"

"Dr. Silva and Gideon are going to take turns keeping watch over you until we kill this thing."

"And where will you be? Hey ... where did you stay last night?"

"I stayed at Dr. Silva's."

"With Mara."

"Yes with Mara. Dr. Silva's house is enchanted. A Watcher can't enter without being invited. I'll be safe there."

"Safe? Who's going to keep you safe from Mara?"

"What's that supposed to mean?"

"It means that she's had trouble keeping her hands off of you, is all."

"Malini, we talked about this. I'm not interested in Mara."

Dane whistled loudly through his teeth. "Stop fighting, you two. Malini, everyone at this table knows that Jacob is in love with you. For Christ's sake, he just about took my head off for suggesting I take you to prom."

Malini straightened in her seat and looked down at the table.

"Yeah, and let's not pretend any of us are going to get our way against Dr. Silva and Gideon. If they say you need protection, you get protection," Jacob added.

"And to be perfectly honest, if they were offering, I'd take some protection, too. Let's all remember what we're dealing with here." Dane pulled the sleeve of his shirt up, revealing the scar where the bone had ripped through skin, a reminder of the beating he'd taken from the Watcher who'd influenced him—Auriel. "She's still out there somewhere, maybe closer than we think. And I'm not exactly on her list of BFFs."

Malini covered her face with her hands. Jacob's arm wrapped around her shoulders and pulled her into his side. With a deep breath, she calmed her nerves and lowered her hands to the table.

"You're right. We all need to make sacrifices. This is bigger than all of us," she murmured. She stood and turned for the door.

"Malini?"

"It's almost six. I've got to go, Jacob. I'm not even supposed to be here."

With both of them staring after her, she left, feeling drained of everything but her will to get beyond this. She stomped to her car and slipped behind the wheel, but didn't start the engine. Instead, she allowed the tinted windows to shield her from the outside world and permitted herself to feel what she couldn't in front of Jacob and Dane.

The tears came then. A few slipping down her cheeks before growing into face-drenching sobs. There was a hole inside of her. The binding that held her together had cracked and the stuff she'd always counted on to glue her pieces back in place was leaking uselessly into her blood stream. Fizz … pop … bang. She could feel her chemistry changing.

"Tell me what I'm supposed to do," she screamed to Heaven. It wasn't a prayer. It was a tantrum. Her fists hit the steering wheel in a rage that seemed to blossom from the inside out. "What am I supposed to be?" The question bounced off the windshield. "What's the big secret?" Her fists pounded hard enough to leave bruises. "If you want me for your team of Soulkeepers, bring me on, but stop messing with my life!"

She closed her eyes and rested her forehead against her fists on the steering wheel. When that position became uncomfortable, she leaned back and allowed her eyes to wander down the row of main street businesses. They settled on the sign for Laudner's Flowers and Gifts.

In her rearview mirror she saw Jacob and Dane emerge from McNaulty's. She wiped her eyes, worried they'd want to talk again when they saw her car was still there. But they didn't turn toward her. Dane walked in the direction of Westcott's grocery and Jacob crossed the street toward his uncle's shop.

"Where are you going, Jacob? We don't work today?" Malini wondered out loud, then remembered. "Paycheck."

She wiped her face off with a Kleenex from her glove compartment. Maybe if she hurried she could catch up with

Jacob and get hers, too. It was a perfect excuse to explain why she was running late to her father.

Chapter 13
Breakthrough

Jacob entered Laudner's Flowers and Gifts wanting nothing more than to grab his paycheck and get out of there. He was worried about Malini and needed to talk to Dr. Silva about what was going on.

"Mom? John?" he called toward the back room. Odd, there was no one at the front counter. Usually when the door opened and the bell chimed, someone came running. Jacob walked past the display of tulips and the cooler of cut arrangements. Whoever was working today must be preoccupied. He pushed open the swinging door to the back room.

What he saw behind the door made him stop so fast his sneakers squeaked against the marble. An icy prickle climbed his spine. On the stainless steel worktable, his mom was unconscious, bound, and gagged.

"Mom!" Jacob rushed forward but he didn't make it to her. A knife stabbed into his left shoulder from behind. He screamed and turned toward his attacker, tearing himself free from the blade. Blood soaked his shirt and dripped to the carved stone floor. He reached out with his power and called the water to him. There was plenty. It exploded out of the vases and ran to his right hand, just in time to shield him from his attacker's next blow.

The knife careened off the disc of ice that formed in front of him. "Katrina! Stop! What are you doing?" he yelled as her face came into view behind the knife.

"I'm killing you, Jacob," she said. Her voice sounded raspy and her face was so pale she looked like a walking corpse. "Now hold still so I can finish the job." She dove forward but Jacob transformed the shield into a blade and swept her arm up, deflecting the blow.

"Why are you doing this?"

"You killed Mordechai. Did you think you'd get away with it forever? The Dark Star is coming and when he does, there will be one less Soulkeeper to get in the way."

She stabbed at his stomach. He brought his good arm down to block her thrust. His left shoulder protested. Blood loss was making him woozy and sweat broke out on his upper lip, but he forced himself to remain standing.

He circled left, toward his mom. Was she even still alive? "Katrina, this isn't you. You're not a killer. You're being influenced by a Watcher, a fallen angel. Once you stop taking whatever it's feeding you, you're going to regret this."

Her mouth twisted into a sneer and a hollow laugh bubbled up her throat. "Stupid Horseman. Everyone's a killer. It's just a matter of what's worth killing for."

She pounced, connecting with his right arm and sweeping his weapon above his head. Her body slammed into him. He rolled backward, meaning to somersault onto his feet, but she clung like a parasite. Searing pain blasted through his torso as he smacked the marble under her weight. Katrina's knife was at his throat. The black blade pressed under his Adam's apple. Sharp. Cold.

Her face inched forward, until their noses almost touched. "This knife is obsidian, Horseman. You do know what happens to a Soulkeeper killed with an obsidian knife?"

"No. What?"

"No Heaven. No Hell. Obsidian kills you and your soul."

Jacob didn't have time to consider the possibility. The door chimed. Katrina's head snapped up and Jacob smashed the heel of his hand into her nose as hard as he could. Even in his weakened state, the force should have incapacitated her, but it did nothing more than temporarily dislodge the knife from his neck. The small shift in power was enough. He punched the hilt and the blade skidded across the floor. Wedged beneath her, he grabbed her wrists and yelled, *"Get out! Whoever you are—run!"*

Katrina broke free of his grip. Her hands shot around his throat, choking the words off. He pulled at her wrists but she was so strong, stronger than she should have been, and he was tired. Tired enough to give in to the darkness that was pressing in all around him. There was blood everywhere. He was bleeding out. He was dying.

Glass shattered against Katrina's temple, and water, blessed water, washed over Jacob's face.

"Get off of him!" he heard Malini yell.

Jacob tried to force Katrina back but he was pinned under her. Worse, he was helpless as Katrina's hand shot out and grabbed Malini by the ankle, yanking her off balance. He expected Malini to tumble backward, but instead, she folded forward, screaming, and caught her weight on Katrina's shoulders.

Malini's scream morphed into a howl of pain. Katrina joined in with equal intensity. From the place where Malini's palms met the bare skin inside Katrina's collar, smoke billowed. The smell of burning flesh filled the room. For a moment, the two stared at each other, as if the skin contact was torture. Then Katrina's body fell forward, face first onto the marble, breaking contact with Malini's hands.

Oily black tar bubbled up from Katrina's back. It dripped from her spine to the floor, twisting into a humanoid shape, until finally solidifying into a boy with a pierced nose and black spiky hair. The leathery black wings that extended from his back left no room for error. He was a Watcher and he had been inside Katrina.

"You!" he hissed and backed away. His shoulders were torched. Black scaly flesh hung in flaps from the muscle. The illusion of the boy flickered in and out, revealing the scaly black skin of the Watcher underneath.

Katrina rolled to her side. "Cord?" she mumbled. She passed out.

Jacob tried to move. He tried to call the water to his aid, but he was too weak. His whole body was icy cold. He'd lost too much blood.

Malini looked in shock. Her hands were charred, covered in black and red blisters. She fell to her knees on the stone floor. The Watcher in front of her was squinting, searching her face like it was memorizing every feature. *Cord.* Katrina had called him Cord. Circling one hand in the air in front of her, Cord captured Malini's image inside a ring of magic. The outer circle glowed purple in the air before the image collapsed into his taloned hand.

"Until we meet again, Healer," Cord said. And then he folded into a ripple and disappeared.

Malini's weeping intensified. She was losing it. Jacob needed to do something to snap her out of her panic. Katrina and his mom were as good as dead and he might pass out at any moment from loss of blood. She was their only hope.

"Malini, you've got to call Dr. Silva," he managed. "Call now, before the Watcher comes back!"

She turned wild eyes toward him, her entire body trembling.

"Now, Malini!" he commanded with what little of himself he had left. And then he let go of his tenuous grip on consciousness and slipped into the impending darkness.

Chapter 14
The Messenger

The sun on Malini's face woke her, the bright warmth soaking through her eyelids. She'd made it to the phone and dialed Dr. Silva's number before passing out from fear and exhaustion. The call must have been answered because there was something soft beneath her and the feel of sheets against her skin. She rolled onto her back and opened her eyes.

"Gideon," she said when she realized it was not the sun at all but the light from an angel that was hitting her face.

"Yes, it is I, Malini."

She looked around at the antiseptic white of the walls and bed linens.

"Am I in the hospital?"

"Yes. The staff here believe you were injured when the Laudners' shop was robbed," he said.

She pulled her arms from under the covers and looked at her smooth, healed skin. "Did it really happen? Did a Watcher come out of Katrina?"

"Yes, Malini. And the rest of it."

"Is Jacob okay? Lillian?"

"Both are recovering well. Jacob needed blood but they've patched him up and he's feeling better today."

"What about Katrina?"

Gideon's face soured. "The Watcher sustained itself by eating her from the inside out. Of course to the humans here, the condition looks a lot like sepsis, so they're treating her as such. She's in a coma in the Intensive Care Unit. I've been visiting her, but the stuff that's inside her is resistant to my healing. It's pure evil that has tainted her veins."

"So, since I'm not burnt anymore, can I go?"

"No, Malini. Dr. Silva has built an illusion around you to make it appear that you are still injured. You will heal slowly over the course of three days. You must stay here during that time."

"Why? Where is Dr. Silva?"

"She would like to visit but it is uncomfortable for her to be in your presence at the moment. And until you learn to control what you are it is possibly dangerous."

"Dangerous?"

"You've been called to become a Healer, Malini. A very powerful one by the looks of it. And you must remember that as reformed as we know she is, Abigail lives in the body of a fallen angel. Now that your power has awakened, physical contact will result in the burns you experienced."

"So, it's true, then? I'm a Healer."

Gideon tilted his head. "Not exactly. Not yet. But you are the seed from which a Healer might grow. Actually, I suspected you were from the start but Abigail wanted to exhaust all other possibilities—"

"You knew? And you didn't tell me?"

"We didn't know for sure and—"

"All this time I've been tortured wondering what I was, if there was even a name for it, and you two knew and let me go on like that…" Her voice broke and her vision blurred. She turned her face into her pillow.

"Malini, Healers are very rare. Abigail and I have only met one, the medicine woman from Peru."

"Jacob told me. He went to see her last year. She gave him a red stone that he gave to me."

"This one?" Gideon held up the necklace that Jacob had given her at Christmas.

"Yes. But, why do you have it? I've stored it in my jewelry box since Christmas."

"I hope you don't mind that I retrieved it. Being an angel does have its benefits in a pinch. Tell me, Malini, why didn't you use this when Jacob gave it to you?"

"He said it told the future and I've always thought knowing the future was a bad idea."

"Why?"

"Because you might do things differently. You know, move against God's ultimate plan. Like, say you saw yourself falling down the stairs and so you avoided the stairs and never fell. You would go on about your life as if nothing ever happened. But what if the reason God had you fall was that when you went to the hospital, you would meet someone, someone that would change your life forever, maybe for the better. Then, by avoiding the fall, you have avoided the change. What if that person was your soul mate or the CEO of a record company that wanted to make you a famous pop star?"

Gideon chuckled in that low bass rumble that was so endearing.

"Seriously, Gideon, I know it sounds ridiculous but I think sometimes it's better to not have control over our future. I would have never come to Paris if I had the choice but then I would have missed out on Jacob."

The angel's face grew serious. He took Malini's hand in his and the warmth from his touch filled her with a kind of giddy happiness. "You are wise beyond your years to trust in God's plan for you, Malini, but as a Healer you must lead the Soulkeepers into the future. You can no longer be a blind follower.

"This path has been laid before you and this stone has come into your hands for a reason. The medicine woman gave this to Jacob, but I don't think it was a coincidence that he gave it to you. It's your time, Malini. You need to discover what it means to be a Healer and I believe the key to unlocking your gift lies within this stone. Who better to train a Healer than another Healer?"

"Oh." Malini sat up and hugged her knees to her chest. "That's what this is all about, isn't it? Dr. Silva didn't want to admit I was a Healer because you two can't train me. There's only one person in the world who can and she lives in Peru."

"This must be difficult for you to accept," Gideon said.

"Hell yeah. I can't get my parent's permission to go to prom. How the hell am I going to go to Peru?"

Gideon placed the red stone into her palm. "I think the Healer thought of that and sent you the means to reach her from where you are."

Malini ran her fingers over the smooth stone in her hand.

"You have three days. Dr. Silva has built an illusion that will conceal any odd behavior as long as you are in this hospital. But you are scheduled to be released Friday morning. When that happens, you must be fully in your mind. Do you understand what I am saying to you?"

"Not really."

"You will." Gideon backed toward the window, into the light that streamed through the blinds. "I'm going to go now, Malini. Don't waste anymore time. Use the stone. Find out who you are. We'll be here when you return."

"But—"

The light pierced through Gideon's flesh like a hundred laser beams, spreading and expanding until he dissolved completely. She was left alone in the room, the red stone pressing a cold circle into her palm.

Chapter 15
Horsemen

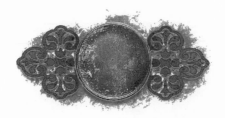

Jacob woke in a hospital bed with one single thought: he had to save Malini.

"Malini," he rasped. His sandpaper tongue stuck to the roof of his mouth.

"She's not here. But don't worry. She's safe. She's with Gideon in the next room."

Jacob turned his head toward the voice and saw Mara leaning against the wall next to the window. She was watching the bag that hung on the pole next to his bed with a sort of disturbed curiosity. Jacob made the mistake of following her line of sight to a half-full bag of blood that dripped into his IV. He leaned back into his pillow, feeling a little queasy.

"It's the second one. You lost a lot, I guess. Dr. Silva says you're going to feel sapped for the next couple of days. Our power comes from our blood and yours is … um … diluted."

"Where is Dr. Silva?"

"She's with Lillian."

The memory of his mom tied up and unconscious on the steel table swept through him. "Is she okay?" he asked.

"Yes, but she was drugged. Dr. Silva worked up a potion she's been slipping her to counteract the Watcher's poison. They're saying she needs to stay until her blood is completely clean. Dr. Silva says maybe a week."

"And the Watcher? Did you catch the Watcher that came out of Katrina? My God, is she even still alive?"

"No," Mara said, then waved her hand when Jacob's face paled. "Don't freak, okay? Katrina's alive—barely. I meant, no, we didn't catch the Watcher. It's still out there somewhere. I'd like to believe Malini scared it back to Nod for good but Dr. Silva says now that it knows what Malini is, it'll be back with reinforcements."

"Now that it knows what Malini is? What is she?"

"Didn't you see, Jacob? You were there. I heard she fried that Watcher when she touched it."

"So, she's a Horseman. She can produce fire."

"No, Jacob, she's a Healer! She burnt the Watcher because what she's made of is so pure she can't touch one without the evil sizzling under her fingertips. She can't even touch Dr.

Silva! Gideon said she's been the first one in over one hundred years. If she survives, she'll be a new hope for us all."

Jacob didn't like the sound of that. He pushed himself up in bed and tried to swing his legs over the side. "I need to see her," he insisted.

"Not gonna happen, hosehead. She's working out the kinks with Gideon. No one can see her for three days. She's got to go on some vision quest to fully manifest her powers. I know you're worried but there's nothing we can do."

Jacob leaned back and twirled the corner of his blanket around his finger.

"And since you don't seem to remember yesterday all that well, I should also tell you that your blood opened up some sort of door at the Laudners' shop."

"What?"

"When your blood dripped onto the floor, it filled the grooves of the carving in the marble and that triggered some sort of trap door. Dr. Silva had a hell of a time hiding it from the police. Don't worry, no one looked down there. 'Your blood, your door,' she said. Plus, we didn't have enough time or yeah, I probably would have checked it out."

Jacob's jaw wouldn't remain closed. "My blood opened up a secret door in my uncle's flower shop?"

"Yep."

"When can I get out of here and check it out?'

Mara paced the length of the room, her arms folding across her chest. "I don't know but I have a hunch the blood has to finish first."

They both eyed the chamber below the bag, the drip-drip painfully slow through the tiny tube. Jacob sighed. He'd just have to wait. But with the Watcher out there somewhere, how much time did he have? How much time did any of them have?

Chapter 16
The In Between

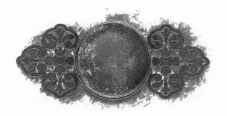

Malini sat up in bed and dangled the red stone from its leather strap. Light reflected off the facets, drawing her eye toward the center, toward the place where the red was so dark it was almost black. It was hypnotic how the stone turned, reflecting her image then absorbing it into its depths. Red, everything was red, and her mind slipped away into that weightless space between sleep and awake. The black center seemed to swallow the red, engulfing her until she was surrounded by nothingness.

The void didn't last long. From the bottom up, a room of multi-colored fabric shingled itself around her. Reams of material draped from vertical spools shoulder-width apart as far as she could see. To her left and right, the rows continued into shadow, but ahead of her the path was illuminated from beyond. She walked toward the light.

Eventually, she heard a swoosh-swoosh, like someone was sweeping the floor in long strokes. Malini turned left at the next ream, following the sound up the row. The fabric was spaced farther apart in this section, opening to a cleared area with a dirt floor and stucco walls. A woman sat at a loom. Tall and dark, her sleek black hair fell almost to the floor. It was the shuttle she heard, sweeping between the threads, back and forth by the woman's hand. Malini didn't have a loom stashed away in her room or anything, but even she could tell the weaving was exceptionally fast, machine-like. A fine, silky cloth shimmered to life where the thread came together.

"Hello, Malini, and welcome. It's about time you came to visit me." She was Indian like Malini and wore a traditional sari of blue and green fabric that shifted as if it were a living organism every time she moved.

"Where is this place?" Malini asked.

"In between."

She didn't think that was a very good answer but moved on to her next question anyway. "How do you know my name?"

"You are a smart girl. You tell me."

"Jacob and Gideon said the stone came from the medicine woman. Are you her?"

The young woman laughed. "The medicine woman is two-hundred-fifty-eight years old." She turned her face directly toward Malini, her hands never stopping their work. Malini inhaled sharply at her beauty: long graceful lines, perfect skin, plump lips, and her eyes, they danced as if lit from within. "I am much older," she said.

Wait, her eyes *were* lit from within! Malini saw the glowing silhouettes of people going about their daily living, pinpoints of light bustling about the world within her. Malini drew back, placing her hand over her pounding heart. She looked around the shop, at the miles of shimmering fabric.

"I know who you are," she said.

"Of course you do."

"You are Fate."

"That is one of my names, yes. You may call me, Fatima."

"Is that why I am here, then? Are you going to tell me my future?"

"No. Not even I can tell *you* your future. For you, I am only a guide and a warning."

"But Gideon said the medicine woman would train me. He said this was an initiation."

"This is an initiation but not the kind Gideon thinks. Gideon has never been here. He doesn't know. Every Healer's experience is different."

"Then why am I here?"

"For you to become what you were born to be, you must face and overcome your greatest fears. You must release what you desire most, and you must choose your course based on your wish to serve, knowing you may do so alone."

"And what if I can't do those things?"

"You are the third Healer born and called. The first two failed the test."

"What happened to the other two?"

"One is dead. The other is in an insane asylum in Israel. Would you like to see?" She leaned in, spreading the lids of her right eye with her fingers.

"Um ... no thanks. I think I get it."

"Oh, I'm not sure you do or possibly could. But then, that is the way it always is at the start. Do you choose to try, Malini, or would you prefer to return to your life as you once were?"

Malini thought about the question. While it was true she often wished her life would be normal again, she knew if she returned it wouldn't change the truth, only her ability to do anything about it. Whether becoming a Healer would be a blessing or a curse, she wasn't sure, but it was better than wondering what could have been, what she might have meant to the world if she would have succeeded. "I'll do it. I want to try, Fatima."

"Very well. To begin, you walk out through the veranda and take the path into the forest."

"Alone? You said you would give me guidance."

"You are wearing it."

Malini looked down at herself and realized her clothing had been transformed into a green sari, made of the same strange material as Fatima wore. It shimmered, lit from within like Fatima's eyes. The red stone was around her neck rather than dangling from her hand as it had been. It glowed like a Christmas bulb.

"I give you this as a gift, so that you remember you must go back to move forward."

Malini waited for Fatima to explain.

"I'm afraid I must get back to my weaving and it is time for you to move along. You have three days. The stone around your neck holds your life force. It will gradually lose its glow as you proceed."

Malini waited patiently for more information. When none came, she spread her hands in disbelief. "That's it? That's all the help you are going to give me?"

"That, and a warning."

"Yes?" Malini stared expectantly at Fatima.

"What you are about to experience is both truth and illusion, the in-between world and the magic of the stone. Make no mistake. If you die on this journey, you die in real life and nothing can bring you back. Follow the path. Face the three challenges and return here before the stone turns black. Or don't, in which case I will say my goodbyes now. Goodbye, Malini."

And then her attention turned to her loom. Malini stood in stunned silence until it was clear that she was wasting precious time. The swooshing sound of the shuttle flying between the strands ushered Malini out onto the veranda and into her future.

Chapter 17
Down Under

Jacob sat up on the side of the bed and gulped down another glass of water. Then he started working at the tape around his IV.

"You can't do that," the nurse said, pressing his shoulders toward the mattress. "The doctor says you need to stay under observation until tomorrow."

"I'm fine. Listen, I'm feeling much better. I need to go."

The nurse shook her head and blocked him with her body.

Mara placed her hand on the nurse's shoulder. "Listen, Nurse Ratched, isn't there some kind of form he can sign about leaving against medical advice or something?"

"My name is Judy, thank you very much. If Jacob was an adult, yes, but as a minor he can't leave without the consent of his guardian."

"Then you better skedaddle and call his guardian. I think that would be a better plan than physically assaulting him in his bed."

"What?"

"That's what I saw. You were pushing him down against his will. Isn't that against the rules, Judy?"

Judy's face turned red and a scowl twisted her mouth. "I'll call your uncle," she said flatly and walked out of the room with more than a little stomp to her step.

"How did you know to say that?" Jacob asked.

"I'm a nursing aide, remember? The first thing they teach you is you can't touch anyone without their consent or the consent of the person responsible for them. She shouldn't have been shoving you like that and she knows it. She wouldn't have tried that with an adult."

Jacob's fingers worked faster against the tape. "Let's get out of here before she comes back."

"Here. Let me." In one motion, she ripped the tape out with the IV attached.

"Crap, Mara, that hurt!"

"Sorry, here." She pressed a square of gauze the nurse had left on the windowsill onto the spot of blood that bubbled up and taped it into place.

"Better?"

"Yeah. Hand me my clothes."

Mara tossed him the bag that was hooked behind the door and politely excused herself into the tiny attached bathroom. Jacob pulled his clothes out of the bag and was pleasantly surprised they weren't covered in blood. Someone had replaced the ones he wore yesterday with a new set. When he was dressed, he knocked on the bathroom door and Mara came out.

"Thanks for the clothes. It would have been hard walking around town covered in dried blood."

"Don't thank me. Your Uncle John brought them after Dr. Silva suggested it."

"She can be very persuasive," he said, cracking a smile.

"I've noticed. Let's get out of here." She peeked out the door into the hall. "We've got an audience. We're going to have to do this the old reliable way."

"How's that?"

She held up her bell and reached for his hand.

To Jacob, one of the interesting things about Mara stopping time was the sound of the bell ringing. If he was holding her hand, he heard the tinkling chime, an innocent, soft sound that seemed utterly unimpressive. But the times when she had used her gift and he wasn't touching her, he didn't hear it at all. It made him wonder whether the bell stopped time or if the magic was in her intention to ring it. He thought about asking her if she knew how it worked but there was so much about his own powers that he didn't understand. He didn't want to put her on the spot.

Mara wove past patients and visitors frozen in various states of movement and led him into the parking lot.

"My truck!" Jacob said.

"Another thing to thank Dr. Silva for," Mara said.

He climbed into the cab and Mara rang the bell again before releasing his hand to circle to the passenger's side. Time continued on. Ten minutes later, he was parked downtown and walking up the sidewalk to the Laudners' flower shop. A hand-written sign on the door said, *Closed, Due to Family Emergency.*

"It's locked," Mara said. "Your aunt and uncle are at the hospital with Katrina."

"My turn to use old reliable," Jacob said. Unfortunately, his water flask hadn't been in the bag with his clothes. He jogged to the truck and pulled out the water bottle he always kept in his cup holder. Using his hand, he channeled the water into the keyhole, freezing it as it went and triggering the mechanism. With a turn of the ice key, the door opened. He and Mara slipped inside and Jacob locked the door behind them.

The corners of Mara's mouth drooped. She reached into her jacket and thrust an orange-flavored sucker that she found there into her cheek. "I can still feel it in here. Can you?"

Jacob *could* feel it. He couldn't smell it like Malini, but the air seemed thicker and all of the tiny hairs on his arms and the back of his neck stood on end. It was the kind of thing he might not have noticed before he was a Soulkeeper. "Yeah. I can tell."

"The door is in the workroom. Come on."

"Wait. Can I ask you something?"

Mara nodded.

"What's with the suckers?"

"They help me focus and they're better than cigarettes."

Jacob couldn't argue with her logic. He followed her into the backroom but there was nothing to see. The room was as tidy as he'd ever seen it. Even more so, the usual dust that accumulated behind the row of plants on the counter had been cleaned up. He looked down at the carved emblem of a man riding a horse with a bouquet of flowers in his hands. The grooves and surrounding floor shined with the effort of a recent scrubbing.

"There's nothing here," Jacob said.

"It's an illusion. Here, Dr. Silva gave me this. Rub it on your eyes." Mara pulled a small pot, the size of a lip balm, from her pocket. She gouged out a portion and rubbed it on her eyes. He took it from her and rubbed some on his own.

At first everything seemed blurry, like he was looking through wax, but slowly the room came into focus, a very different room than he'd been in a moment ago. It looked like a scene out of a horror movie. There was blood everywhere. Most of it was dry but in some places it was so thick that it still had a wet gleam to it. There were scuff marks on the table where the straps had bound his mother, and telltale scratches where the metal buckles had scraped the stainless steel as she struggled. The dust was back behind the row of plants.

But, he also saw what he came there for. The emblem, grooves filled with his blood, was slightly sunken. Hinges were visible on one side, as was a half-inch gap on the other.

"Dr. Silva didn't go down there?"

"We didn't have time. The police were on their way."

"You have all the time in the world. You own time. Why didn't you go down?"

"I offered. I wanted to, but Dr. Silva said, 'no.' Your blood, your door, remember? She was afraid that if anyone besides you went down there, it might be a trap. Especially for her. Who knows what your great-great-grandfather had in store for a Watcher who spilled your blood."

Jacob shook his head. "How would my grandfather even know what a Watcher was?"

Mara's brow furrowed and she lowered her chin incredulously. "Jacob, your great-great-grandfather was a Soulkeeper."

"No, I get it from my mother's side."

"Do you even go to science class? It's a recessive gene. A chromosome from your mother and a chromosome from your father must combine to create a Soulkeeper. Your mother is a Soulkeeper, so that meant you would receive at least one Soulkeeper gene from her but the second one had to come from your father, and he inherited it from his father, who inherited it from his father, who had it because your great-great-grandfather was a Soulkeeper."

"Okay, I'm buying the genetics part but how do you know it was my great-great-grandfather? It could've been anyone in my father's family tree."

"I don't. But Dr. Silva does. She says she knew him when he was alive. It's how she knew you'd be coming someday. He left this for you, Jacob."

He was about to argue when he remembered the conversation he'd had last year with Katrina. Their great-great-grandfather's last will and testament required the shop be left to a male Laudner heir. If he understood correctly, the man had gone to great lengths to ensure the Laudners couldn't deny the provision. The legal arrangements were airtight. It never made sense to Jacob why a man would do such a thing. But if his great-great-grandfather had somehow known that Jacob would come and that he would be a Soulkeeper, then it all made sense. If this was left for him, it was something important.

"I'm going in," Jacob said, moving toward the sunken spot on the floor. He pushed on the emblem and the marble panel swung inward, revealing a three-foot drop and a winding staircase.

"I'm coming with you," Mara said, stepping in close to his side.

"It's too dangerous. We have no idea what's down there."

"Better that I go first then. I don't have anyone waiting for me at home."

Jacob stopped, hit by the blatant honesty and sadness in her words. That was the thing about Mara, she had this hard sarcastic exterior like she could rip his head off both literally and figuratively. Then she would blast him with a piece of personal history that made him feel so sorry for her he'd do almost anything to make her feel better. "We go together," he said firmly. He reached up and took her hand, helping her drop into the passageway.

"We need a flashlight," Mara said. "No, wait, there's a lamp on the wall. We just need to light it."

"John keeps a lighter for the votive arrangements. Hold the door. I'll get it."

Jacob ran to the front of the store and grabbed the lighter from behind the cash register. He dropped into the hole after her, flicking the switch and lowering it to the dusty wick of the oil lamp. First one lamp came to life, then a line of them one after another. The lamp oil drew the flame down the passageway, igniting lamp after lamp until the flame turned the corner beyond what he could see. Jacob took a few steps downward and allowed the door to close above him.

He swallowed. "Only one way to find out what's down there."

"After you," Mara said.

He descended the spiral staircase, running his hand along the cold, stone wall. When he could see the landing at the bottom, a breeze blew up, causing the flames to flicker. "This must lead outside. I was wondering why it wasn't stuffy in here after being closed up for so long."

"Weird," Mara said flatly.

Jacob reached the landing and emerged inside a vast cavern filled with the most beautiful white sand. About thirty feet away, hitched to a stalagmite, was an old-fashioned wooden sailboat, the sail stowed away.

"Do you think there used to be water here?" Jacob asked.

"Seems like it. I doubt that sailboat was always wedged in the sand like that. Maybe in 1850 the water table was higher." Mara squatted down and ran her fingers through the sand. "Wow. It's soft. I've never seen sand like this."

"There's nothing else here. Do you want to check out the sailboat? Maybe there's something inside?"

"Sure."

Climbing over the side of the boat, he soon discovered there wasn't much to see. Two wooden benches stretched across the hull on either side of the boom and behind the mast. There was no rudder and only one sail. Jacob tugged on the outhaul. The canvas sail rose slightly. A warm breeze blew through the cavern, stirring up the sand and tousling Jacob's hair.

"What are you doing?" Mara shifted uncomfortably on the wooden bench.

"I'm going to raise the sail," Jacob said. He yanked the outhaul more purposefully. Halfway up, the breeze in the cavern grew to a solid wind worthy of a thunderstorm.

"I have a bad feeling about this, Jacob," Mara said, clinging to the side of the boat as her ebony hair whipped across her face.

Jacob ignored her. On impulse, he hoisted the sail into position and tied it off. A *chug-chug-chug* like an approaching train echoed through the cavern. Jacob's eyes widened as the reverberation became deafening and the wind accelerated to the point where he gripped the side of the boat as dutifully as Mara. "Hold on!" he yelled to her but his voice was muffled by the growing storm.

It came like an explosion. A forceful ball of fire rolled through the cavern, bouncing off the back wall and pounding into the open sail. The boat shot forward like a rocket, coasting across the sand and sending waves of it spraying up on either side of the boat. Jacob ducked down low, as did Mara, mouths open in screams that were lost in the power of the blast.

Jacob tried to watch where the boat was going but the walls of the cavern were nothing but a blur. He braced himself for the inevitable collision with the end of the cavern and closed his eyes tightly to stop from getting ill. But several screams later, the boat slowed, and he opened his eyes. They weren't in the cavern any longer. The sailboat floated under a pristinely blue sky.

"Mara, look!" he yelled.

The river beneath the boat was Caribbean blue, the water carving through miles of white sand toward an oasis. At the tree line, there were two enormous statues of angels, swords crossed. When Jacob passed under them, an endless fire arced over his head, licking up the swords from hilt to tip of blade. Jacob had the eerie feeling he was being watched. And then an intense pressure squeezed the breath from his lungs, pinched in some invisible grasp. He had the impression he was being sifted, his cells passing through a membrane. The weird feeling passed as quickly as it had come.

The boat entered the oasis, and a paradise of tropical trees made him forget about the feeling. Colorful birds darted above him and the climate was as perfect as any he'd been in, including Hawaii.

The sailboat docked itself at a sandy beach. The sail rolled down and stowed itself away on its own. Jacob tied the rope to the long bamboo dock and helped Mara out.

"Where do you think we are?" he asked.

Mara shrugged, chewing the remainder of her sucker and stowing the stick in her pocket. "There's a path." She moved toward the place where the trees parted.

Jacob followed. The whole environment reminded him a little too much of the deadly garden that used to exist in Dr. Silva's backyard. Wary and alert, he scanned the plants for anything that seemed capable of drawing blood.

"Chill out, Jacob. You're making me nervous. Stop acting so … twitchy," Mara said.

"I've learned not to trust anything that looks too beautiful."

"Is that why you're with Malini?" Mara snickered.

Jacob jerked like he'd been punched in the gut. "For your information, Malini is the most beautiful thing I've ever seen. I do trust her and she trusts me. But her beauty is authentic. You can't compare her to people who've altered themselves for some ill-conceived notion of what others think is attractive." As he said it, he made a point of focusing on her pierced lip.

"I was just joking, Jacob. You don't have to be mean." She advanced more quickly down the path, pushing branches out of her way as she went.

"And neither do you," he said. "You've had a problem with Malini since the moment you got to Paris. Why?"

"Let's just say, in my experience, she's the type of girl who gets everything she wants."

"And what exactly is that supposed to mean—" Jacob cut off his question abruptly because, as Mara pushed aside a palm frond, the sight of a plantation-style mansion came into view. Under a tiled roof, a series of white archways welcomed them.

"There's a sign," Mara said. She walked over to the wooden square that had long been overgrown with leafy vines. "I need something sharp."

Jacob pulled the water bottle from the pocket of his hoodie and produced a dagger. He sliced through the vines and Mara swept them away with her hands. He stared, speechless. The sign read: **The Eden School for Soulkeepers Est. 10,000 BC**.

"There's a school for Soulkeepers?" Jacob asked.

"Not anymore by the looks of things. I don't think anyone has been here in decades."

"Let's go inside."

Jacob led the way, cutting across the overgrown prairie that used to be a yard and stepping up onto the veranda. There were two oversized wooden doors with iron pulls. He took one and Mara the other. The doors swung open with the rusty screech of disuse.

The foyer they entered made the Taj Mahal look like Motel 6. Every color of the rainbow glinted in the sunlight that cascaded through the doors. The walls were encrusted with gold and gemstones.

"Holy expensive taste, Batman." Jacob gawked at the jewel-encrusted depiction of Adam and Eve standing under an ornate tree on the ceiling.

Mara sighed. "Adam and Eve don't look anything like I pictured. They're short. And Adam is ... lacking."

"Lacking?"

"That's an awfully small fig leaf, don't you think?"

"Mara!" Jacob laughed. He was going to say it was an artist's depiction and not necessarily accurate, but then stopped himself when he realized it was quite possible whoever built this school knew exactly what Adam and Eve looked like. "Should we look around?"

"We should."

He led the way toward the hallway to his left and opened the first door he came across. Inside, the classroom looked like a modern chemistry lab. "What the hell? This stuff looks fairly new?"

From one of the lab tables, Mara picked up a beaker. "The bottom says it was manufactured in 1950."

Jacob pulled open the drawers of the desk at the front of the room. Nothing. He hurried to the next room. This one was filled with old-fashioned school desks: old fashioned as in 1960's style, not Flintstones era.

Mara ran to each one, lifting the top and running her hand inside. "They're cleaned out."

Jacob tried the teacher's desk, opening all of the drawers. Within the center drawer Jacob felt a tiny corner of paper trapped in the joint. He slid his hand in and pinched it tightly, then pulled. It came slowly, like a printer with a paper jam, inch by inch from between the wood and metal. Finally freed, the typed piece of paper made his stomach twist.

"They had classes in Detection, Combat, Poisons and Antidotes, History of Good vs. Evil … Mara, this is a class schedule. They were teaching Soulkeepers here. What happened to this place? Why did they stop?"

"I don't know, Jacob. The man who trained me, he said that at one time there was a council, a group of retired Soulkeepers and religious leaders that helped organize the Soulkeepers. He said they disbanded. He never explained why."

"Dr. Silva never told me anything about a council."

"What would be the point if it didn't exist anymore?"

In a silent funk, Jacob worked his way down the hall. There was a dojo for martial arts training, fully equipped. How much his mother would have appreciated that as a new Soulkeeper! There was a lecture hall with what looked like a skeleton of a Watcher on display near the podium. At the end of the hall, a flight of stairs led them to the second floor.

"These look like offices," Jacob said, peeking in the open door of the first room. There was a wooden desk and bookshelf of dusty tomes.

"Jacob, I think you should see this."

Jacob turned to where Mara was standing across the hall. She was staring at a plaque outside the door to an office. This room was bigger than the others and the leaded glass in the windows led him to believe whoever worked there was someone important. Jacob squinted at the copper plaque, reading through the tarnish.

Warwick Crusaford Laudner, Provost. "Mara, does this say what I think it says?"

"Yes, Jacob. Your great-great-grandfather ran this school."

"Damn."

"Hmm. What you said."

Jacob ran his finger along the letters. When they didn't offer up any answers, he walked around the open door into the office. There was a desk facing the door that was obviously for a secretary. It was empty. Behind it was a closed door decorated with stained glass. Jacob reached forward and turned the knob.

Mara laughed. "I feel like I'm breaking into the principal's office at school. I hope we don't get detention."

Jacob ignored her and pulled the door open. Inside, the office was opulent. A multi-tiered shelf full of crystals and stones in all shapes and sizes stood at the back, filtering the light as it came through the window. A map of the world stretched across an entire wall and an enormous and intricately carved desk rested in front of a leather chair in the middle of the room. There was a piece of paper centered on the desk. He turned the yellowing page toward him.

"It's a note from my great-great-grandfather. It's a notice to all Soulkeepers."

"What does it say?"

"It is with deep regret that I must announce the closing of the Eden School for Soulkeepers. The low numbers of Soulkeepers born to our world and the high mortality rate have forced those of us who teach here to join those who fight on the other side. Effective immediately, all living Soulkeepers, including teachers, council members, and students, will report to the front lines. If we should be successful in these dark times, it will be because we acted with courage and virtue, united in our singular goal. The beast must remain chained. God have mercy on our souls. Sincerely, W. C. Laudner."

"My God, Jacob, how bad must it have been? For them to leave this place, give up their safety, their entire structure. How close were we to complete Watcher takeover?"

"Couldn't have been that bad, right? We're still here. They must have been successful."

"Yeah, but they aren't here. They're dead. You know, before Dr. Silva, I had never met another Soulkeeper besides my Helper, Mr. Bell. I'm still not sure how Abigail found me. How many Soulkeepers do you think there are left?"

Jacob blinked in her direction, the words rumbling through his head. "We should go back. We need to ask Dr. Silva."

Mara became freakishly still, as if a current of electricity was rooting her to her spot.

"What's wrong?" Jacob asked.

"Don't you think it's strange that Dr. Silva has been around for more than a lifetime but she never told you about this? She said she knew your great-great-grandfather. It seems like an important piece of information to overlook. Unless she wanted to leave it out."

"What are you saying?"

"I'm saying, maybe Dr. Silva isn't as trustworthy as we think she is."

"Don't be stupid. She didn't try to hide the trap door from me."

"She couldn't. I'd already seen it."

"She's done nothing but help me. And, she's helped you. She found you. She's letting you live in her house."

Mara frowned. "You're probably right."

Jacob strode out the door and into the hall. Mara followed at his heels. "We should go back. We should ask her about this. I'm sure there's an explanation."

"Yeah, plus I'm guessing the hospital has noticed you missing by now. The Laudners are probably wondering where you are. We don't want them asking too many questions."

"Agreed."

Jacob hurried out of the building and back down the path to the dock, Mara following close behind. He folded the letter and tucked it in his jeans pocket next to the schedule. Mara crawled into the boat, taking a seat near the bow. Untying the boat and stepping in after her, Jacob raised the sail. This time, when the fire and wind launched them back into the cavern under the Laudners' shop, he knew what to expect. But it wasn't until he dropped onto the sand and stood on the dark, lamp-lit landing that Jacob realized where he'd been.

Breathing the heavy air, the weight of an evil world settled on his shoulders. The change was both physical and emotional. All his fears and insecurities returned at once.

"We were in Eden," Mara said, shoulders sagging.

Jacob felt the loss that was apparent in her words. Eden was perfect, like being immersed in pure light. He hadn't appreciated it for what it was until he'd left.

He paused, resting his hands on his knees until his body adjusted to being in the real world. When he'd recovered, he helped Mara climb the stairs and emerged into the blood-covered back room. Jacob wondered if the wistful nostalgia he felt for Eden was one tenth of what Adam and Eve had felt the day they were cast out forever.

Chapter 18
Vision Quest

Through a stucco archway, Malini exited the warehouse of fabric. The *swoosh-swoosh* of Fatima's weaving faded as she crossed the veranda and took her first steps onto the path that led into the forest. At first the trees were far apart, like an English countryside or a city park. Hours passed and the landscape darkened, overcast by trees that crowded the path and twisted into each other overhead. With the dark came mist and moss that hung like gray beards from the tangled limbs. The air grew thick and her slippers squished with every step on the now muddy pathway.

It wasn't long before she recognized she was in a swamp. Ahead, the path ended at a body of water, coated with algae.

She inched her toes closer to the edge and wondered how she might get across. Her sari was supposed to provide guidance. She looked down at the shiny material and doubted its usefulness. "Unless it can help me walk on water," she whispered.

She took one tentative step forward. Her slipper sunk through the green slime to the mucky bottom. "Nope," she said and pulled her soggy foot back to shore. Retreating a few steps, she held the cloth closer to her face, wondering what type of guidance it could give.

A tickle on her shoulder made her drop the cloth and swipe her hand over the spot. Fur and legs! "AHHH!" She swiped the spider from her sari. It scuttled off but more dangled above her head from eerily invisible webs. They were tarantula fat, some as large as a salad plate and all getting a little too close for comfort. "Eww," she said, brushing her fingers over her hair frantically to check for more. She backed away until her heels touched the edge of the water.

"Deepest fears. Yep, spiders are one of them, which means—" She turned to face the water again and saw a patch of scaly skin a foot wide break the surface. "Snakes. Large, venomous snakes." She was talking to herself, which may have been a sign she was going insane from fear, but it helped to hear a voice say it, even if it was her own. Calling out the obstacles always helped her overcome them.

On the far bank, the path picked up again. Obviously, her first test was to get across. Then, who knew? To her right, an eye the size of a basketball broke the surface of the water. The snake was watching her. Instinctively, she stepped back from the water's edge.

Malini's heel stepped on something rubbery—a spider. Behind her, more spiders dropped to the pathway and approached her with hungry eyes. There were thousands of them. A creepy-crawly itch prickled across her skin, but when she looked there was nothing there. She searched the trees for a vine, a branch, anything that might help her.

A few feet to her left, a rotting log jutted into the swamp. With a leap, she landed at its base, brushing the spiders that had crawled onto her legs into the water. The murky depths churned where they fell. They did not resurface. The other spiders stopped at the water's edge, presumably fearful of the predator within.

Malini shuffled down the log anyway, aware that the eye that had been watching her had sunk back into the swamp and the current around the log was uneven, as if something large waited just below the surface.

The *boom-boom* of her heart threatened to knock her off her perch. The other bank was too far away to reach without wading through the water and going back was not an option. Hundreds of spiders now crowded the roots of the fallen tree, thousands of eyes locked on her every move.

"Guidance," she stammered. She ran her hand over her sari again. "I need help!" she cried. No one answered. She was alone. At the hem of her pallu, the loose end of the sari, she felt a thread hanging. Without thinking, she peeled it off with unsteady fingers.

A bead of sweat fell from her forehead. She placed the thread across her palm, wondering what Fatima had meant about the fabric being her guide. What made the material special? It was so hot and humid that her head swam as she tried to examine the fiber. She dug her toes into the bark to steady herself.

Concentrating on the thread, she became aware that the shimmer was caused by alternating light and dark pieces along its length. On ... off ... on ... on ... off. Maybe it was a code, like how a computer reads pulses of electricity. But how could she read it? The answer came quickly on the question's heels. As she focused on the fiber, the pulsating light wrapped around her body and pulled her into the thread.

With a jolt, she found herself in a clearing on the edge of a jungle. The ground was sandy, broken by the occasional mound of green brush. A tiny Indian girl looked out over the landscape.

"Hello?" Malini said. The girl did not respond. Reaching out, Malini tried to shake the girl's shoulder, but her fingers passed right through.

"Wisnu!" the girl called. Her voice was urgent, worried.

An older woman approached, a basket on her hip. "Come, Avantia. It is time to go."

Malini startled at the name. Avantia was the name of her great-great-grandmother.

"We can't go, Mama. Wisnu is missing."

"Who is this Wisnu you are talking about?"

"My pet. The lady gave him to me."

"What lady?"

"The old lady in the jungle. She gave me Wisnu."

"We have no room for pets, Avantia. Let the woman keep her strays. We don't need another mouth to feed."

"Don't worry, Mama. He lives outside and he hunts his own food. Wisnu! Wisnu!"

"Stop playing. It is time to go. Baba will be angry if we are late."

The girl stomped her foot. "Not without my Wisnu."

At this the older woman snatched the child's wrist and dragged her toward the two ruts that Malini assumed served as a road. Avantia followed behind obediently, weeping and mumbling, "Goodbye, Wisnu."

Abruptly, Malini came out of the thread and back into her head. Bending her knees, she struggled to maintain her balance on the rotten log. What kind of guidance was that? A child calling for an invisible pet? She placed the thread into her pocket with a huff and wiped her head with the back of her hand. So hot.

Before she knew what was happening, the log beneath her feet crumbled inward, its rotting flesh unable to hold her weight a moment longer. She dropped into the swamp. Thankfully, the water wasn't deep. Her feet hit bottom. Popping her head above the surface, she raced, half running, half swimming for the opposite shore.

The thick, scaly body of the snake wrapped around her waist. She tried to push it away, but in seconds it had coiled around her, ankle to chest. The head came around to face her, and she looked into the yellow eyes of the thing that had been watching her. Taking a deep breath, she tried to make herself as big as possible. She knew how this would work. Once she exhaled, the snake would tighten. Unable to inhale again, she would suffocate and the snake would eat her. She had only one breath left. She had to use it wisely.

"*Wisnu!*" she screamed as loud as she could. It was her only hope. She had to trust that Fatima had given her the sari for a reason and that the piece of history she had seen would be somehow useful. Her breath gone, the snake constricted. It rolled her under the water with bone-crushing strength.

Malini didn't bother to struggle. Beneath the murky depths, she tried to clear her mind, to accept death with dignity. The light of the red stone flickered as she sank to the bottom. The snake's open mouth approached her head.

To her surprise, the vise around her waist loosened. She was thrust to the surface. Gasping for air, she forced her crushed and aching body to shore. On nothing but adrenaline fumes, she propelled herself onto the delta of sand. Air entered her lungs in hungry gulps. She searched the swamp for the miracle that had freed her.

What she saw filled her with dread. A gigantic rat had attacked the snake. Razor-sharp teeth flashed. It locked its jaws around the reptile and Malini watched grayish-brown fur and scaly skin tumble into the water. All Malini could think of was how the scene reminded her of a Godzilla episode. Would she be the tasty prize for the winner?

Spiders, snakes, and rats: the hellish trifecta of terror. The horrific din of the monsters battling in the swamp ended. By the shreds of reptile littering the shore, Malini guessed the rat had won. Would it come for her next?

Tears boiled up and spilled down her cheeks. She tried to run, but her body wasn't ready and she crumpled to the pathway. She tried again, succeeding to drag herself a few blessed lengths up the path. But the surge of adrenaline had used up everything she had. Her muscles refused to work for one more minute. Closing her eyes, she waited for the rat to attack, and tried to stop the uncontrollable trembling that had overtaken her body, despite the languid heat.

Something warm and wet slid up her cheek. Her eyes popped open. There was a mousy snout touching her nose, and two dark brown eyes that looked crossed, they were so close.

"Gah!" She startled backward in the sand.

An uncommonly long pink tongue jetted out and up the side of her face, over her ear.

"Eww." The tongue was gross but the rat wasn't gnawing on her. She pushed herself to a seated position. "Either you're friendly or you're tasting me. Which is it?"

In response, the creature, which was roughly the size of a tiger, sat on its haunches.

"I'm going to presume friendly. You aren't a rat at all, are you?" She could see more of him now and the spotted tail that was beginning to dry on the bank of the swamp. "You're a mongoose. I've been saved by a giant mongoose." She giggled and the animal jumped to its feet and turned in a circle at the sound.

Then an idea flashed in her mind. It was an idea so crazy she almost didn't want to say it out loud. "Are you Wisnu?" she asked softly.

Of course, she didn't expect an answer, but the mongoose stepped forward and bowed.

"It is you. You're Wisnu. Wow, saved by my great-great-grandmother's magical pet mongoose. I did not see that coming." She reached forward and scratched Wisnu behind the ears. "I guess this is what Fatima meant about going back to go forward."

Wisnu lowered his entire body next to her. She wasn't sure how she knew, but she had the sense she should climb on, that Wisnu wanted her to ride him. The spiders in the branches above her were the only encouragement she needed. She accepted Wisnu's invitation and climbed onto his back, burying her hands in the fur near his neck.

He was off. Malini clutched his pelt to keep from falling off as he bounded down the trail. Soon the trees thinned and Wisnu paused on an emerald-green plain. Malini slipped from the animal's back and stretched out on the grassy knoll, grateful she'd escaped the swamp.

Finding herself in relative safety, she gave in to the pressing exhaustion. Her last thought before drifting off was of Wisnu keeping guard beside her.

Chapter 19
Confrontation

Thankfully, the Laudners were quick to forgive Jacob for leaving the hospital without permission. They were probably too exhausted from keeping vigil at Katrina's bedside night and day to worry about their healthy nephew. Katrina wasn't any better and the doctors were hesitant to give a prognosis. So, after a brief scolding, they let Jacob off the hook.

Later, across from Dr. Silva in her parlor, Jacob finished telling the story of Eden for the second time. Mara glared at Dr. Silva with pit-bull resolve. She wanted answers. None were forthcoming.

Dr. Silva clutched the schedule and letter in her hands. She leaned back in her chair, tapping her foot nervously. Jacob had long given up on trying to follow her darting gaze.

"How can this be? I've never heard of this in all my generations. Gideon? Did you know?" Dr. Silva asked tentatively.

Gideon paced in front of the fireplace, a habit that was becoming all too familiar to Jacob. His wings twitched. The air around him crackled. Jacob had never seen him so agitated. "No, I did not. But you must remember we are not of Soulkeeper blood and you were called to this role after Warwick's lifetime."

"Did they all die?" Mara asked. "How many Soulkeepers are left?"

Dr. Silva shifted in her chair. "I've always thought only Helpers trained Soulkeepers. I knew of your great-great-grandfather, Jacob. I even suspected he was a Soulkeeper. But never did I suspect he was part of something like this. A school! For Soulkeepers! And a council!"

"Dr. Silva, answer the question. How many Soulkeepers are left? You must know. You must have a way of finding them or you wouldn't have found me." Mara pushed a piece of hot pink hair from her forehead. She locked eyes with Dr. Silva and Jacob shivered at the aggression that was in that look. Mara wasn't afraid … of anything.

"I didn't know, until recently," Dr. Silva whispered.

Gideon, who'd resumed his pacing away from her, turned on his heel. His eyebrows knit and his lips parted.

"I suspected what we were dealing with when I saw the reports of the missing. It's not just Chicago, Mara. It's everywhere. No one likes to talk about it. You humans think it will always happen to someone else. I know better. This new activity reeks of Watcher."

She spread her hands as if there was nothing more to say.

"Spill it, Abigail," Mara said.

"I knew something was going on and I needed to pull a team together to investigate. But when I visited the medicine woman and asked for names, she wouldn't give them to me. She said the time wasn't right for me to organize a larger team of Soulkeepers. But I knew ... I knew Jacob wasn't ready to do this alone, even with Lillian's help."

"And, so? How did you find Mara?" Jacob asked.

"I conjured the list with sorcery."

"No!" Gideon dug his fingers into his hair. Heat and light rolled off of him like he was radioactive. "Why, Abigail?"

"I don't get it," Mara said. "What's the big deal? Why does it look like your head's about to explode?"

"Abigail walks a space between Heaven and Hell. She has access to things through her sorcery that no other can rival. To use that power against the advice of the medicine woman is pure folly and she knows it. Our Healer is our only hope in these dark times," Gideon explained.

"So, you broke the rules. You conjured my name. So what?" Mara asked.

"I conjured all of their names."

At this, Gideon sat down on the leather recliner so hard Jacob thought it might buckle under the force. "That's how they know. That's why the Watchers know who they are! You brought knowledge into the temporal realm. How could you not realize that Lucifer could reach it here? How could you not realize he would be watching you, waiting for you to make a mistake?" Gideon glowed brighter. Jacob leaned away from him.

"It needed to be done!" Dr. Silva snapped. Her eyes flashed in a way that couldn't be mistaken for human. "The medicine woman is ancient. She's out of touch with contemporary society. She didn't give me a prophecy and she certainly didn't give me a mandate. She simply wouldn't help me. Don't you see, Gideon? Organizing the Soulkeepers would mean she might have to leave the Amazon. She's two-hundred-fifty-eight years old! Don't tell me it wasn't self-serving for her to deny me. Don't tell me she wasn't hoping I would wait until the next medicine woman passed her initiation. Hell, she might have known about Malini."

"You don't always know better, Abigail. We have roles for a reason." Gideon smashed his fist into his palm.

"We don't know for certain they have the list. I put a very strong Nocturous spell on it. For all we know, they were bluffing. Lucifer knows the list was conjured. He might not know who is on it."

Mara held up a finger. "They have to know. They came after Jacob."

"They already knew who Jacob was. He killed Mordechai last year in Nod. We knew they would come for him sooner or later. But the fact Katrina passed Lillian up the first time she tried to kill you means the Watcher inside of her didn't know what she was initially. That could mean they can't read the list."

Jacob rubbed his temples, his mind reeling. He tried his best to sort out everything he'd just learned.

"I saw that thing, the Watcher who came out of Katrina, take some sort of picture of Malini before it escaped. If they didn't know what she was from the list, they know now. She's at the hospital alone. Someone needs to protect her. They'll come after her for sure." Jacob rose to his feet.

"I've enchanted her room. No one can reach her, only the illusion. She's not there anyway, not really. She'll be gone for three days and if she comes back, she'll be a true Healer. She'll be more powerful than all of us," Dr. Silva answered.

"What do you mean, if?" Jacob said through his teeth.

Gideon and Dr. Silva exchanged glances. "There's no easy way to tell you this, Jacob. The reason the medicine woman is over two hundred years old is because the last two Healers did not survive their initiation. Malini has everything she needs to survive but if she chooses not to trust in the gifts God has given her, she will die."

Jacob swallowed hard and fell back onto the sofa. To prevent sprinting out the door, he clutched the plaid fabric. She wasn't there, not really. And he couldn't protect her this time. He leaned forward and buried his face in his hands. He tried to accept that this was one journey she had to complete on her own.

Mara reached across the coffee table and grabbed Dr. Silva's wrist. "How many are there, Abigail?"

Dr. Silva frowned at Mara's grip. "There were thirteen on the list. Three Helpers, not including myself or Gideon, nine Horsemen, and one Healer. Thirteen Soulkeepers."

Mara dropped Dr. Silva's wrist and cupped her fist in front of her lips. "That's it? We need to hold back the tide of Hell with fifteen people?"

"No," Dr. Silva said. "Thirteen people, one angel, and me."

Chapter 20
At Death's Door

Malini awoke to Wisnu's wet tongue lapping up the side of her head. He alternated licking her face and nudging her shoulder. Once she was fully conscious, she understood the why behind the alarm clock routine. The stone's glow was noticeably dimmer.

She pulled herself to her feet feeling achy but better than before. The bruises she should have had from the snake's choking grip didn't exist. From the outside, she didn't look hurt at all. On the inside, well, she refused to give those feelings a voice just yet.

Wasting no more time, she continued her journey down the dirt path. Eventually, she could make out a magnificent stone castle on the horizon. She climbed on Wisnu and urged him forward, closing the distance to the castle at a high run. But when he'd reached the garden in front of the stone steps, the mongoose stopped, pinned his ears against his head, and growled in the direction of the dark fortress.

"I think I'm supposed to go there, Wisnu," Malini said. "I don't like it either but Fatima said I need to make it to the end of the path and the path leads straight to that castle."

Wisnu turned in tight circles. Malini slid from his back. "It's okay, Wisnu. Thank you for your help. I'll go on from here."

Head hung low, he trotted off. Malini followed the path through the garden and up the stone steps to the gigantic iron door. She lowered the heavy brass knocker three times. The *bang-bang-bang* seemed to echo across the countryside. There was a moment of silence and then the door swung open.

No one stood on the other side. Past the entrance, a grand foyer of black marble rose above her. At the center of the room, a table held a vase filled with long-stemmed red roses. Their heady smell filled the air, the color an uncommonly bright red against the black walls.

"Hello?" Malini called. She took a step into the foyer and noticed the marble floor was discolored where her feet fell. The path continued even here. On the table with the roses, a note waited for her.

Take one, she read. She reached out and pulled a rose from the vase before continuing forward. The path led her into a great ballroom.

"Welcome, Malini," a voice said, hollow and cool. A boy stood at the south end of the ballroom, a tight-lipped smile across his face. Dark brown hair swept across his forehead above eyes a shade of brown that was almost black. His pale skin stretched smooth over beautiful, almost feminine features. The tux he wore hung like it was custom tailored. He looked familiar, like someone famous, but Malini couldn't place him.

"Time to get dressed for the ball, Malini." He snapped his fingers and the rose melted down her arms like liquid mercury. When the red touched her sari, it transformed into a strapless red ball gown.

Freaked, Malini clutched at the bodice. Without her sari, she was completely without guidance and she had no idea what this challenge would entail. "Who are you?" she asked.

"You look stunning. Would you like to see?" the boy said, ignoring her question.

A mirror materialized at the center of the room, its gilded frame an intricately carved masterpiece. When she stepped over to it, her feet clicked against the floor. She lifted the full ruby skirt to find four-inch heels had replaced her slippers. Glancing into the mirror, she realized that wasn't all that had changed. Her hair was swept up high on her head with cascading curls brushing her cheeks and neck. Her lips were painted as red as her dress and her makeup made her look older than she was. The medicine woman's red stone was mounted on an elegant gold chain around her neck.

"What is this about?" Malini asked, turning to see that the top of the gown was a corset, tied tightly in the back.

"This is a ball, and we are here to dance." He clapped his hands and a man appeared and sat at a grand piano that she hadn't noticed when she'd entered the room. The boy met her eyes and bent at the waist, extending his hand toward her.

"I can't dance," she said.

"Oh, I think you know this step," he whispered.

Tentatively she took what he offered. His fingers slipped in, as cold as death against her palm. The pianist began a heavy waltz and the boy pulled her into his chest. He led her across the floor, step-step-spin, step-step-spin, and she did know the steps as if it was a dance she'd danced every day of her life.

"I have a gift for you, Malini. It is His will that you have a piece of what I am. It is a powerful gift and I do not give it lightly."

"Who are you?"

"You know who I am, Healer. I am the thing you hate the most. I am the thing you mistake as your enemy when truly I am the world's most important blessing."

Malini felt dizzy, almost nauseous. The turning, the cold press of his skin, the music that was eerily strange. She stopped and he followed her lead although he did not release her right hand. The pianist played passionately, his fingers flying across the keys. But *holy hell* she was watching his performance through his back! His body was opaque, dressed in ghostly clothing that reminded her of something from the seventeenth century.

"He's not alive." Malini's throat constricted and the words came out as breathy whispers.

"No," the boy said.

His icy grip tightened around her fingers. "Oww," she said. "My fingers are going numb. Do you mind?"

"An unfortunate side effect of my gift, I'm afraid," he said.

A moment of clarity allowed her to see the room for what it was, not a ballroom but a grand funeral parlor. The flower arrangements in every nook, the melancholy dirge of the piano, the cold marble: this was a house of the dead.

The coldness advanced to her wrist. She could no longer feel her hand. The ghostly pianist continued to play, but the cadence of his music transformed into grief in D minor.

"You are Death," she rasped.

"Yes."

"But I don't understand. Have I failed? Am I going to die?"

"I am here to give something to you, not to take something from you," he said, pulling her back into his chest. He forced her to continue the dance. Step-step-turn, step-step-turn.

Her forearm was frozen, icy numbness creeping toward her elbow.

He locked eyes with her, spinning her round and round the room. Those black eyes began to burn and in them she saw all manner of death: fire, pestilence, war. They were like Fatima's eyes, windows into the history of the world, but with a much darker view. Round and round he danced with her, toward the mirror at the center of the room. And then, without asking permission, he lowered his mouth to hers.

She tried to pull away but his arms held her tight to his body, his lips pressed to hers in an icy cold kiss. The chill filled her, the numb extending from her mouth to her throat, to her cheeks, and on to her toes until her speeding heart slowed, giving itself over to the deep freeze. But it was her arm that went completely numb. She could no longer feel it at all.

And then he was gone. She opened her eyes and felt the warmth return to her face. Her heart started to beat again. She turned a circle looking for the boy but he'd vanished, as had the pianist and the piano. The only thing that remained was the mirror.

She looked into it and for the first time noticed what death had given her. Raising her right hand, the one that had gone numb, she stepped closer to the glass. She bent and released her fingers. But they were not fingers. The flesh of her arm ended at the elbow and her hand was nothing but skeletal bones that clicked as she moved them.

The skeleton arm flexed and stretched. She couldn't help herself. She screamed and tugged at the place the bones joined her elbow as if she could rip the arm from the joint. Echoes of her terror bounced back at her from the marble walls.

Death had given her a piece of himself. She had the hand of death. Collapsing to the floor, she held it away from her body, weeping. Why? What kind of gift was a hand of Death for a Healer? Would this follow her back to the real world?

After she ran out of ideas for getting rid of it, she accepted that the skeletal arm was a part of her, at least for now. The stone at her neck flickered. She was running out of time. Determined to continue, she left the ballroom and followed the path to the door on the far side of the castle. There, on a small table, was a brown glove with a note pinned to it.

"Use me," she read. "How very 'Alice in Wonderland.'" She slipped the glove onto the bone hand. Once it was on, it transformed to match her skin. She let herself out, hoping never to return.

Death's voice came to her through the closing door. "Thank you for the dance." The words held nothing but genuine gratitude. Malini thought she heard loneliness in those words. She didn't stay to find out if she was right.

As she ran down the hill, she was grateful that the gown had been replaced by her sari and slippers and surprised that the red stone remained set in its cocktail splendor. When she realized Wisnu was waiting for her at the bottom, she threw her normal arm around him. Into the furry bend of his neck, she buried her face and cried.

Chapter 21
Practice

Going to school without Malini sucked. Jacob rested his head in his hands over his uneaten lunch and tried to keep himself awake. He'd tossed and turned all night wondering if she was okay. Whatever the Healer initiation was, according to Dr. Silva, it was deadly. Of course, it seemed like everything in the Soulkeeper's world was deadly. That's why they needed a school. Soulkeepers needed to learn from each other, especially if Watcher activity was on the rise.

"Earth to Jacob!" Dane waved a palm in front of his face.

"Wassup, Dane?"

"Wassup? You look like the walking dead, that's what's up. And where is Malini? What the hell is going on?"

Jacob met Dane's eyes and couldn't hold it in. He needed to talk to someone or he was going to explode. "There was a Watcher in Paris. Malini—"

Jacob stopped because Dane had jumped to his feet and was holding his fork like a weapon.

"Dane, sit down. She's okay … for now."

"I want to know what happened," Dane said, returning to his seat.

Jacob ran a hand down his face. Why did he start this? It wasn't the time or place to be sharing the details.

"She's fine, okay? And it's gone for now. But, my God, Dane…" Jacob paused, gauging Dane's reaction. "Are you in love with my girlfriend?"

"No!"

"Then why are you acting like you're about to jump on a white steed and ride to her rescue?"

Dane's hands clenched into fists on either side of his orange tray. "You don't get it, do you? I would act the same way if it were you."

Jacob shook his head. "Yeah, right."

Dane leaned forward and whispered across the table, "How do you feel about Dr. Silva and Gideon, Jacob? How do *you* feel about the people who saved you from *them*, those … things?" He straightened in his seat but didn't break eye contact.

When he did think about it, he understood where Dane was coming from. There wasn't anything Jacob wouldn't do for the people who had saved him from Nod. He never thought about it before, but he had done the same for Dane. He was the one who saved Dane from Auriel's wrath.

"You two are the only two who understand why I still wake up at night. And the only two who can tell me if I really have something to be afraid of."

"I guess I get your point," Jacob said. He thumbed the corner of his tray, thinking that they'd far exceeded the depth of conversation he was comfortable with. Dane must have felt the same way because he shifted uncomfortably and became preoccupied with the window.

Eventually he found a topic to fill the awkward silence.

"So are you coming to the meeting after school today?" Dane asked.

"What meeting?"

"Prom committee. It's just around the corner. We're voting on a theme today."

"Sorry, I can't. I'm supposed to spar with Mara. Dr. Silva says it will be good practice in case the Watcher comes back."

"Fine. You go save the world. I'll deal with the prom."

"What themes are you thinking of anyway?"

"Um, I've thrown out a few to the group. Zombie apocalypse, NASCAR, sports legends ... but the girls weren't crazy about them. Besides Malini and us there's only senior girls on the committee. I dunno, I think zombie apocalypse was growing on Bridget Mason."

"There's nothing like a few decaying body parts to make for a romantic prom," Jacob added.

"I know, right?"

* * * * *

After school, Jacob met Mara in Dr. Silva's backyard. He only had an hour to practice. He'd promised the Laudners he'd take over in the store tonight so that John could go back to the hospital. Katrina's status had improved slightly in the last twenty-four hours but she remained unconscious.

"Thanks for coming," Mara said. She must have sensed him because she didn't turn around when she said it. Sitting on the garden bench, she stared toward the raised beds, her long black hair braided down the back of her head.

"No problem. Where's Dr. Silva?" Jacob asked.

"She's checking on Malini with Gideon. She should be done with her initiation tomorrow afternoon. Dr. Silva just wants to check her body."

"To make sure she's still alive," Jacob added gravely.

Mara turned then, her blue eyes catching the light. "Yes."

Jacob moved toward the house, slipping his backpack off his shoulder. A heavy weight settled over his heart. Hopefully, the training would distract him from the constant worry. He tossed the pack down next to the greenhouse and gathered himself together. "So where do we start?" he said.

"Dr. Silva wanted us to spar. I guess we just attack each other. Don't hold back. We need to simulate how a Watcher would fight."

"She's trying to get us ready. She knows it's just a matter of time."

"But we've known that since Chicago, Jacob. Why do you think she's encouraging this now?"

Jacob thought about the question. His eyes burned with fatigue and he rubbed them with his thumb and forefinger. "I think it's Malini. She's a Healer. One of only two in the whole world and now they know who she is. I think Dr. Silva knows they'll try to find her. I think they want to end her before she knows what she's doing. If they have some kind of plan, if you believe the Watcher's warning, she is the only one of us who will know how to stop them."

Mara twisted a tendril of hair that had escaped her braid around her finger. She seemed to be weighing something in her head.

"Let's get started." She walked around the bench and squared off against Jacob, the bell in her hand.

"So, we use our full powers. No holding back?"

"Kind of," Mara said. "Technically, I could stop time and thrust something sharp through your gut. Game over. But a Watcher can't do that, so neither will I."

"Thanks."

Jacob reached out with his power, to the puddle that collected under the drainage spout. They bowed to each other and the fight was on. The water flew to Jacob's hand, his sword cruising in her direction. She leapt into the air and the weapon passed beneath her feet. And then she was gone.

Jacob tried to react but her arms were already bear hugging him from behind. He threw his elbow into her gut, forcing her backward. She let go.

In the blink of an eye, she was in front of him again. He brought the sword around. She disappeared. A foot caught him in the ribs and he went flying, tumbling across the back lawn. He flipped up to his feet and charged at her, tossing a sharp disc of ice in her direction. She disappeared again.

His only hope was to get close enough to touch her. If he was touching her and she stopped time, he'd stay animated with her. She reappeared behind him and wrapped her arm around his neck in a chokehold. Big mistake. Within her arms, he twisted to face her. She broke away and Jacob saw her move to ring her bell.

Lurching forward, he grabbed her wrist. Time stopped around them but, because of the contact, he didn't stop with it. She struggled to free herself, twisting and hurling her other arm at his face. But he abandoned his sword, allowing it to drop to the earth, and blocked her punch. She tugged backward, ringing the bell again, and Jacob felt the air move around him once more. But, he didn't let her go.

Mara's foot shot forward, sweeping his legs out from under him. He tried to shift his weight and failed. Falling to the ground, he pulled her down with him, rolling over until he'd pinned her to the lawn. Hands restrained on either side of her head, she was helpless. He'd won.

"Gotchya," he said.

She stopped struggling. There was a look on her face he didn't understand. It was more than defeat. It was surrender.

"Are you okay?" he asked.

She shook her head slowly, raised it from the grass, and planted her lips on his. For a moment, he wasn't sure what was happening. Her lips were warm and wet and his body responded automatically. Her lips parted. Jacob jerked back, standing clumsily and wiping her kiss from his mouth.

"Mara, I—" he began. The next thing he knew he was lying on his back, his arms pinned on either side of his head. She was straddling him, her body pressed against his, her face so close he could feel her breath.

"Gotcha," she said into his lips. Slowly, she crawled off of him.

Jacob sat up feeling disoriented. His heart was pounding against his ribs, quickened by the sparring and maybe something else. Mara looked toward the horizon, working pretty hard not to meet his eyes.

"Mara, did you do that to distract me?"

The slightest hint of a blush colored her cheek.

"Of course. Why else would I do it?" she said, but her body betrayed her. She crossed her arms in front of her chest and popped her hip out defensively.

"It felt real."

"Well, you obviously haven't kissed very many girls then."

Jacob got to his feet and walked over to the place he'd left his backpack. Slinging it over his shoulder, he thought about just leaving and forgetting it ever happened. But in the end, he couldn't let it go.

"No. I haven't kissed anyone but Malini. But I hope I never kiss so many people that I can fake it as well as you can."

He turned to leave.

"Jacob?" Mara said.

"Yeah?"

"I wasn't faking," she mumbled toward the horizon.

"What?" Jacob had heard what she said but didn't want to believe she'd said it.

She turned to face him. The late afternoon sun glowed behind her head and in the light she was stunning. "I didn't fake it," she said more clearly. "I want to be with you. I've never met anyone who made me feel the way I feel when I look at you. We're equals, Jacob. Can't you see how good it could be?"

He didn't know what to say. His jaw dropped open and his mind went blank. All he knew was her silhouette against the light, the way the breeze and their sparring had loosened tendrils of her black hair, and the sudden electrifying memory of her body pressed against his. She was walking toward him. There was something he should say. There was someone else he should be thinking about.

And then her arms embraced his neck and she kissed him again, a hard, demanding kiss that set him off balance. Her hips pressed into his, her hand dug into the hair at the back of his neck, and Jacob tried to remember why he should stop this, why the kiss and the heat felt good and wrong at the same time. It was a while before he remembered.

Slowly, he pushed her away. "I can't do this. I'm with Malini. I shouldn't have let that happen."

"But you did. You're not married to her, Jacob. If you like me, why not give me a chance, too?"

"I do like you, Mara, and you are ... unbelievably beautiful. But I love Malini. And that means more to me. It would kill me to know I'd hurt her. I'm sorry."

"Yeah."

Jacob nodded a goodbye, straightened the backpack on his shoulder, and walked as quickly as possible to his truck. He was relieved when he climbed behind the wheel and locked himself in. He'd never intended to kiss Mara but he couldn't deny he'd enjoyed it.

The greatest temptation was that he could get lost in her. Kissing Mara, he hadn't thought of Watchers or Katrina or Malini's initiation. He hadn't thought of anything. She was an escape. Mara didn't have a dad who hated him and she was a Horseman, just like him. It would be simple with Mara.

But Jacob didn't love her. He loved Malini.

He started the truck and backed out of Dr. Silva's driveway, disappointed he'd let it go as far as it did. Malini would be home soon. Would he tell her what happened? Could he? Could he live with himself if he didn't? Jacob rubbed his chest where his heart began to ache.

Chapter 22
The Last Challenge

Once Malini regained her composure, she released Wisnu's neck and sat down on a boulder near the path. Raising her right hand, she saw that the glove Death had given her looked exactly like her own flesh and blood. There was a thin pale mark on the crook of her elbow. She dug her finger in and peeled back the glove to reveal the bones.

Wisnu backed away, whimpering.

"Yeah. Imagine being attached to it," Malini said. She flexed and stretched the bone hand in front of her face. Next to her, a patch of violets bloomed. She reached out. One slight brush and the flowers shriveled to a crispy brown. Near her foot, a spider scampered toward Wisnu. Malini, who had even less love for spiders after the first challenge, touched it with a skeletal finger. It died, the legs curling into the abdomen.

Could she touch herself? She must be able to if she was attached to it. She tested it out by removing her slipper and tapping her little toe. Besides the odd feeling of bone touching skin, nothing happened.

Malini slid the glove back on and frowned. She was exhausted. Gauging the time of day by the sun was impossible; there wasn't one, just an undefined glow that filled the sky. She wondered how long she'd been there. What day was it? The stone was black around the edges now, with only a soft glow at the center. She had to keep moving.

On her feet again, she continued down the path. "Come on, Wisnu. We have to keep going." He trotted along next to her, sniffing at her gloved hand.

"Be careful. It's safe with the glove on but I don't want to take any chances."

Wisnu snorted and trotted to her other side. The path changed from dirt, to sand, to pebbles. Malini's feet and legs ached from walking and her eyes burned, her lids heavy. She should've rode Wisnu but by the time she thought of it, they came to a place where he wouldn't go. The pebble path led to a shiny brass gate. Behind the gate, row after row of headstones stretched as far as she could see, and the path continued right up the middle.

"I'm guessing the best time for guidance is before I walk into the creepy cemetery."

Wisnu paced nervously a few steps behind her. The sky grayed with no moon or stars to break the dingy night. Malini felt along her sari for another thread and pulled it free of the fabric. She laid it across her palm. The pulses of light wrapped around her, pulling her into the lesson of her past. It was easier this time, now that she knew what to expect.

She was standing on a cricket pitch. An Indian man and his son were hunched over a stitched leather ball. She recognized her grandfather right away, but it took her a while to know that the boy he was teaching to bowl was her father at eight years old. She had to remind herself that it was called bowling and not pitching like in baseball. It had been a long time since she'd watched someone play cricket.

"Place your fingers like this, Jahar," her grandfather said, positioning her father's fingers wider on the ball.

"But why, Baba?"

"Because this will cause the ball to spin and make it harder to hit."

Her father bowled the ball across the cricket pitch. It bounced and veered left out of bounds.

"The other way is easier," her father said.

Her grandfather growled out a disappointed scoff. "Easy? Nothing worth doing is easy, Jahar. Nothing worth having is easy. You need to learn different ways so you can adapt to the situation."

"You mean I need to throw what the hitter can't hit?"

"Yes. Yes. This isn't just about cricket, Jahar. In life we have to solve the problems we face. We have to think critically about the situations before us. Your education, your experiences, they are all valuable. They create your tools to overcome the difficulties you will face."

Her dad squatted to pick up another ball near his feet.

"Bowl again, Jahar."

"Yes, Baba."

Malini emerged from the vision with a smile on her face. The advice her father always gave her, "solve the problem," it came from her grandfather. She tucked the thread into her pocket, wondering how this vision would help her. "See you on the other side, Wisnu," she said. "I hope." Opening the gate, she followed the path into the cemetery.

Once the gate clanked shut, she was enveloped by silence. The only sound was the shuffle of her slippers on the pebble path. She reached the first row of headstones, but couldn't make out any of the writing in the stone. The grave markers were ancient and weathered, the inscriptions worn away. She continued, watchful.

About halfway across, she smelled the first Watcher. It was perched atop a mausoleum, cloaked in the illusion of a man but with his wings fully extended. He turned to her, his eyebrows rising before he jumped down from his perch.

"What have we here?" he asked. The phrase hung in the air between them. Malini picked up her pace toward the opposite gate. But there were more. Watchers poured out from every corner of the graveyard, closing in around her. Taunting her.

"Looks like lunch to me," a redhead in black leather said. She licked her lips.

"I want a leg," a tall Watcher with a goatee snapped.

"Now, now, Bernard, we all need to share but there will be plenty to go around."

Malini turned in a circle, trembling as she counted six Watchers closing in around her. She wanted them dead. She wanted out of this place. It seemed the perfect time to use her new gift.

Pulling her glove off, she raised the skeleton hand in front of her. "Stay back or die!" she yelled.

"What's this?" a blonde male with stocky muscles said. "Less meat for us." He reached out and snatched the bone fingers, then brought his face dangerously close to hers. "If Watchers were alive, I might consider that a threat." He moved in, flashing teeth.

Her other hand shot up and pushed the Watcher away as hard as she could. The pain was immediate. Her palm sizzled against his flesh and blisters bubbled on his chin.

It backed off. "It burns!" he hissed. This incited the other Watchers and suddenly they were upon her. She reached out, burning one then another, but it was only flesh on flesh that worked, and soon they had figured out that grabbing her hair or sari was much more effective. Everywhere talons clawed at her, ripping, hurting. And then a belt was around her neck. She hadn't seen it coming. The Watcher behind her laughed as he tightened it, choking her.

"Perhaps we can eat it after it's dead," the redhead hissed. Malini worked her fingers inside the strap, trying to hold enough space to maintain her windpipe. Instinctively, she'd used her healing hand, her left. She looked at her right hand, the hand of Death, and thought about her vision. How could she use it differently?

She clawed at the strap around her neck with the bony fingers but they were no more useful than her flesh and blood ones. Still, she could feel something in her bones. Death's hand was buzzing from the inside, as if it knew it had something more to offer.

The belt tightened, cutting off the air to her lungs. Desperate, she reached out to the buzz and asked it with everything she had left to help her. The buzz grew stronger and she bent the bony fingers, pulling against a cord she could not see, beckoning a force that seemed just beyond her reach. She called with her fingers again and again, the buzz growing stronger as she was drawn closer to unconsciousness. The stone around her neck blackened. Was she dying or out of time?

And then the strap around her neck loosened. Air burned down her raw windpipe into her lungs. A spark ignited at her throat, the stone coming back to life. With the newfound oxygen, she was suddenly aware of a commotion going on around her. The Watcher with the goatee struggled against an opponent, someone choking the Watcher from behind, someone tall and strong.

Malini turned in place. An army of people had come to her rescue. Everywhere, the Watchers fought off attackers. She tried to see, to focus on the people who had come to her aid.

One of them was injured. The man's arm hung useless as he scuffled with the red-headed Watcher. Then she noticed another had a rancid wound in his side. As she turned in place, the buzz in her hand was so strong it felt like a swarm of stinging wasps. But she didn't care about the pain. She just wanted out of there.

She backed down the path, toward the opposite gate, sliding between the Watchers and their attackers. It was only after she moved outside the ring of violence that she saw where her rescuers had come from. The graves nearest the scuffle were open, fresh piles of dirt on each one. And farther out, hands were breaking the surface of the graves.

The dead were rising.

Their milky eyes sought her out, awaiting her command. They were hers. She had raised the dead. The bones of the older corpses pulled themselves together, gristle and strips of muscle in various stages of decay. The buzz in her bones intensified with each one who rose from the grave.

"Kill them," she commanded and, with inhuman howls, they did. The zombies ripped the Watchers apart piece by piece. Wings and limbs and heads flew from the fight, and their black blood oiled the path. When all were finished, the dead stood facing her, swaying slightly at attention.

On instinct, she held up the buzzing hand, which had coiled into a fist. "I release you," she said loudly and relaxed her fingers, letting the invisible cord that she had retracted out inch by inch. The zombies walked backward to their graves, sinking into the dirt one by one. When all were buried again, Malini held the hand up in front of her face. She could still feel them there, under the surface, waiting for her next command.

"Holy shit," she whispered, turning the bones back and forth in the twilight. Shivering with the remnants of fear and lingering exhaustion, she found her glove and slid it over the bones. Then she finished walking the path and emerged from the cemetery.

She collapsed to the grass on the other side of the gate. With the adrenaline giving out, the pain hit her full force. A ring around her neck throbbed where the strap had dug in, her limbs ached, and her skin burned. Black and red blisters ran from the elbow above her skeletal hand, across her chest, and down her left arm. She couldn't see, but she suspected by the pain the burns covered her stomach as well.

Every breath was excruciating. She curled on her side and sobbed into the grass. The pain was unbearable. She prayed to die.

When a warm, wet tongue licked her cheek, she knew it was Wisnu. He sniffed her face worriedly. She was too exhausted to respond. Digging his nose under her belly, he rolled her across his neck. A few jarring steps later he dumped her gently into an icy cold stream. The water was only inches deep but it sprayed over her as it jetted across the stones, soaking her to the bone.

"*Wisnu!*" she yelled, getting a mouthful of water in the process. She planted her hands on the bottom and pushed herself up to a sitting position. When she felt steady, she stood and walked her shivering body to the shore. "Wisnu! Bad boy. No!" She shook her finger in his face and the mongoose lowered his head to the grass.

But, Malini had to admit, the pain was better. The blisters faded to pink tender skin and then completely healed. She rubbed her neck and found it free from pain as well. She remembered the day in the lab, when the water had washed her burn away.

"The water heals me! Wisnu, you're a genius!" She wrapped her arms around the animal, hugging his neck and burying her face in his fur. He rested his chin on her shoulder.

When she pulled away, she looked up the grassy knoll near the stream and an odd feeling turned her stomach. The water ... this meant something. The truth came to her without any effort, a sad revelation she couldn't deny.

"I always thought ... When I was a little girl, a Buddhist monk gave me a note. He said it was my destiny. The note read *water*. Since last year, I thought the note was about Jacob. I thought that we were meant for each other because his gift was water. But maybe this is all it meant. Water heals me. Maybe the word didn't mean Jacob at all. Maybe it was just talking about me. About what I needed to be whole."

Wisnu had nothing to say about the theory but he licked her face in response. She ran her hand over his neck, pondering the idea that maybe her love for Jacob wasn't destined at all. Maybe it was a relationship just like everyone else's.

"How about a ride, Wisnu?"

The mongoose lowered his body and Malini climbed on. He jogged down the path while Malini pondered her journey and wondered if she had any energy at all for what was to come. But relief spread across her body when she saw the veranda where she'd begun in the distance. As Wisnu grew closer, she could make out Fatima sitting at a table across from a short, dark woman who looked positively ancient.

The two women stood when they saw Malini, raising their glasses in the air. Fatima spoke in a loud, husky voice. "Hail, Malini, our new Healer, shaman, and medicine woman. You shall give life with your left hand and bring death with your right. Congratulations, Soulkeeper."

Both women drank the red liquid in their glasses and then bowed their heads in her direction. Malini should have felt proud to have succeeded, or relieved to be alive, but instead, as she watched the women beckon her to their table, all she felt was the weight of the world shifting to her shoulders.

Chapter 23
Return

Her body was too warm. That's what Jacob thought when he took Malini's hand in his. She felt feverish. Was this his warning that she wasn't coming back? Jacob had noticed his temperature drop when he called the water, but he'd always assumed it was because he used ice to fight. But when Mara used her power for too long, her body turned icy cold. Did Soulkeepers grow cold at their most powerful? And what did that mean for Malini who was burning up?

He leaned forward from his perch on the end of her bed and placed his lips on her forehead. Then, even though he had an audience of his mom, Mara, Gideon, and Dane, he lowered his lips to her mouth and gave her a proper kiss.

"Come on, Malini," he whispered to her. "Wake up."

He jolted when he felt her hand move. "She squeezed my hand!" he said to the others.

They crowded in around the bed. "Malini? Malini?"

Her eyes fluttered open and Jacob gasped audibly. The normally chocolate-brown color of her eyes was luminescent, a deep golden-brown lit from within. The others in the room leaned in for a better look.

"Oh my God," Mara whispered.

"Wowza," Dane said with childlike astonishment.

Malini swallowed and then her lips began to move. "Water," she mumbled.

The room became a flurry of activity, everyone tripping over each other to grab the foam cup with the straw off the bedside table. The nurses had been caring for her illusion for days, and Jacob felt the ice shift within the cup as he snatched it out of Dane's hand and brought the straw to her lips.

She drank greedily, and then sat herself up in bed, motioning for Jacob and Dane to back off. She met the eyes of each of her visitors. "What is everyone staring at?"

"Gideon, pass her the mirror," Jacob said.

"Of course," he replied, handing the mirror from the bedside table to Malini.

Malini lifted it in front of her face, turning her head from side to side to check out her new eyes. "Well if that freaks you out, then you should all probably brace yourselves." She lifted her right hand and scratched at the inside crook of her elbow. Her fingers caught, and then like something out of a horror movie, she peeled back her own flesh from her bones.

"Sweet Jesus!" Lillian yelled from her spot near the windows. She was still technically a patient and hugged the robe she was wearing tighter around her body.

Jacob leapt to his feet, backing toward the windows. Dane vomited into the garbage can near the bed. Mara pressed herself against the closed door of the room, her eyes wide. Gideon completely disappeared.

Malini laughed. "Look at all of you. It's as if you've never seen the hand of Death before."

In the silence of the room Jacob heard his heart pounding as every cell in his body told him to run. Sure, the sight was horrific, but it was more than that. The thing on the end of Malini's arm emitted fear and dread. The air was heavy with impending doom.

He was relieved when she slipped the flesh back over the bones and flexed her fingers. "It's harmless with the glove on but I wouldn't recommend touching it otherwise." She said this softly, as if she realized any loud noise or sudden movement might push her audience over the edge. Her eyes flicked downward and Jacob saw a frown creep across her face.

"Well … you must have some story to tell, Malini," Jacob said. A smile forced its way onto his face. He returned to her side, leaned forward, and took her into his arms. For all the changes she must have experienced, her hug felt the same.

And the longer he held her, the more the fear drained from the room.

Jacob released her, sliding his hands down each of her arms. They felt normal, the same as always.

"Welcome home, Malini," Gideon said, reappearing near the window.

Dane nodded and patted her on the shoulder.

From her space behind Dane, Mara added, "Welcome back," then slipped into the hall. Jacob's stomach twisted as he thought about kissing Mara. The secret between them already festered like an old wound.

"When can I leave here?" Malini asked.

"This afternoon," Gideon replied. "Your illusion has been progressing nicely and your doctor plans to release you today based on your perfect test results. Of course, all of those were faked as well. I have no idea what your blood would look like at this point. I don't recommend you allow them to examine you too closely from here on out."

"And Katrina? What happened to her?"

"She's still in a coma. We've done all we can. I couldn't heal her." He breathed a deep sigh.

"Take me to her," Malini said. Jacob noticed a change in the way she said it. Her voice, usually soft, took on an almost military charge. No one in the room would have dared say no to her.

Jacob helped her out of bed and wrapped her robe around her shoulders. "Dane, you should wait here. They only allow two visitors at a time."

"Okay," Dane said. Jacob didn't think he was disappointed. In fact, he still looked a bit pale from vomiting.

Lillian led the way out into the hall. They rode the elevator down a level and found Katrina's room in the Intensive Care Unit, next to Emergency. They paused at the glass wall. Carolyn Laudner was kneeling next to the bed, praying the rosary. Katrina's body stretched motionless, her chest rising and falling only with the aid of a ventilator.

Jacob knocked on the see-through door.

"Carolyn, the kids would like to visit with Katrina. Why don't you let me buy you a cup of coffee?" Lillian said. She put an arm around Carolyn, who nodded. Leaning into Lillian as she stood, they walked past Jacob and Malini to get out the door.

Aunt Carolyn paused as she passed, placing a hand on Jacob's shoulder. "Thank you for coming to visit her. I think she knows we're here."

Jacob nodded and walked to the bed, watching his mom usher his aunt down the hall. When he returned his focus to Katrina, all he could think was that Aunt Carolyn was terribly wrong. Katrina didn't know anyone was in the room. As far as Jacob could tell, she was barely alive.

"She's close," Malini said, as if she read his mind. "But we can't allow her to die. She may have information that will help us. We need her."

Jacob wasn't going to argue. Not with the look of certainty on Malini's face. He watched as she approached Katrina and worked her left hand under the gown, onto the skin over her heart. On contact, Jacob watched the heart monitor change. The heartbeat quickened and became more even.

Malini closed her eyes and the room was filled with a smell, like burning flesh. At the place she touched, smoke rose between her fingers. Jacob looked up at the fire alarm and said a silent prayer it wasn't enough to set it off.

Katrina's body twitched. "Is she having a fit or something?" Jacob asked, but Malini didn't answer. She seemed far away or deep within herself, Jacob couldn't tell. What he did know was that thick black goo oozed from Katrina's nose and ears. He'd seen that ooze before. Watchers bled that stuff when you stabbed them.

Black dribbled from her mouth. Black stained the bedspread where it looked like she'd wet herself. Jacob shivered to think that stuff was inside of her. How had she survived so long?

Malini's hand began to blister between her fingers. Black crispy skin creeping up her wrist. Jacob reached for her, but Malini pulled her burnt hand away before he made contact.

"It's okay, Jacob," she said. "This is how it's done." She turned to the little sink next to the bed just as Katrina began to cough around the tube in her throat. Jacob watched as the water from the sink washed away the burnt edges, then the blisters, then the red burn, until Malini's hand was completely healed.

"What the hell?" Jacob said.

Katrina's eyelids fluttered. She gagged and coughed, her hands slapping the bed.

"You'd better hit the button," Malini said.

Jacob realized his mouth was hanging open. He didn't bother to close it, but reached above Katrina's bed and hit the red button marked *emergency*. In seconds, the room was flooded with doctors and nurses. They surrounded Katrina, shouting instructions to each other as she thrashed on the bed.

Within the chaos but not a part of it, Jacob felt Malini grab his hand. He followed her in awestruck silence as she led him out the door.

Chapter 24
The Unreal World

By the time Malini's parents picked her up from the hospital, the other Soulkeepers and Dane were long gone. The most uncomfortable part was that her mom and dad had visited her illusion frequently over the last three days but she had no memory of it. When her mom came into her room, she had the most atrocious yellow sweater from the back of her closet.

"Why did you bring that one?" Malini asked.

Her mother laughed. "Don't you remember? Yesterday, you insisted you wanted to wear it home."

Once again, Dr. Silva helped the way only she could. The medical records had been altered and it turned out Malini had received medication that both explained the temporary loss of memory and her change in eye color. Never mind that it made no sense why the medications were given for her condition. The doctor said he had never seen such a pronounced change before but insisted it was harmless. Her parents accepted this as fact, and that was the end of it.

It was quiet on the drive home and Malini watched her father grip the steering wheel like it was the last hope for the world. His jaw was tight. She thought she could hear his teeth grinding.

"I'm happy to be going home. Finally. I'm probably so far behind in school. It will be good to get back to normal."

"Normal? How can there be normal when this type of crime is taking place in our happy town," her father said. "First Stephanie Westcott goes missing and now this. Maybe we should move."

Malini laughed. "Very funny, Dad."

"I am serious."

"Don't be silly," Malini said. "I'm sure they'll catch who did this. We can't move." A sense of panic washed over her. What would she do if she had to move? How would she handle her responsibilities? "You have your business, Dad!" she threw out desperately.

Her father pulled into their driveway and put the car into park. He turned sideways in his seat to look at her, his eyes glossy with tears. "I would rather lose the business and all of our money, then risk losing my only daughter."

For a moment, Malini couldn't speak. She'd never seen her parents this emotional. "Dad ... I—" She was about to say that she wasn't going anywhere. But she couldn't promise that. At best, she'd be going away to college and at worst, well, she wasn't immortal and all hell was about to break loose and come after her. She chose her words carefully. "Why don't we go inside and talk over dinner? I've missed you guys so much."

Her father relaxed a little. "That's an excellent idea."

Malini climbed from the backseat and followed her parents inside. "Heal thyself, medicine woman," she said under her breath. Her relationship with her father was one problem only she could solve.

* * * * *

The day Katrina came home from the hospital, Jacob and his mother were helping in the Laudners' flower shop. By the time they'd closed the shop for the night and drove home, Katrina was settled into one of the sage green recliners and Aunt Carolyn was trying to spoon soup into her mouth.

"Mom, I can't eat one more bite. I'm fine, really," Katrina said. The truth was, she was more than fine. The doctors called it a miraculous recovery. As Jacob looked at her pink cheeks and bright eyes, all he could think of was Malini. He wondered how much it had hurt, how hot it had burned, to save his cousin. He wondered if she was worth it.

Katrina turned toward Lillian and Jacob. "Hello!" she said cheerfully. Jacob almost looked behind him to see who she was talking to. It was so unlike Katrina to be friendly.

"Um, hi," he said.

"How are you feeling?" Lillian asked, giving Jacob a sideways look.

"Fine. As good as new, actually." She said this while dodging the advancing spoon aimed at her mouth. "Mom, can I talk to Jacob for a few minutes?" she said, pushing the bowl away. "Alone."

Aunt Carolyn looked confused but was still in full spoil mode from Katrina's illness. She nodded and stood up. Lillian lifted the bowl and placed a hand on her elbow. "Carolyn, what do you say we take a walk? It's a beautiful spring night."

"Yes. I think I could use some air," she said absently.

Jacob took a seat in the recliner on the other side of the fire. Katrina didn't speak until the front door closed behind the two women.

"I know, Jacob. I know what you are." The smile had melted from her face and she said the words in a deadpan voice.

"What are you talking about?" he feigned.

"When that thing, Cord, was inside of me, I knew his thoughts. I was still in there. He just had control. It was like I was…" She shook her head and tears started down her face.

"You were possessed, Katrina," Jacob said, softly.

"Yes. But I tried to kill you. I mean, it tried to kill you with my hands." She met his eyes. "I'm sorry."

"I know it wasn't really you, Katrina. I forgive you."

Jacob watched the tension bleed from her shoulders. The firelight danced across her face, her eyes twinkling with far away thoughts.

"They are coming ... Cord and more like him. They have a list of all of the, um…" She seemed to struggle to find the right word. "Soulkeepers, right?"

Jacob nodded.

"Well, they've got a list of all of you but they can't read it. It's like scrambled or something. They knew about you from before and they suspected what Malini was but … Gosh this is so weird, Jacob. It's hard to explain, I was seeing his memories and I couldn't interpret them all."

"Just try, Katrina. It's important. What else did you see?"

"It was Malini they were really after. Cord didn't know who she was until the very end. He just knew she would be near you. It was so weird. When I was attacking you in the shop and she came in, she looked like a ghost to me. I could barely see her until she touched me. Then he knew. Cord knew what she was and that she was what he was looking for. He wanted to kill you but he wanted to find her."

"Do you know why?" Jacob asked.

"No. He was out of my head before I understood for sure. But I think it has to do with the list. I think they want to use her to interpret the list. Then they can find the rest of you, right?"

"Yeah. Actually, that makes sense."

"Will you protect me?" She was crying now, trembling in the chair. "Can you keep it from happening again?"

Jacob had never been close to Katrina, but for all the times he wanted to hurt her, he couldn't stand to see her so broken. "It'll be okay. I'll make sure it doesn't happen again. We're ready for them."

"But I have to go back to school, Jacob! What then? What if Cord comes back?" Her weeping grew in strength and she pulled a tissue from the box on the table between them.

Jacob stood and walked over to her. He squatted down next to the chair and placed his hands on hers. "There's more than just me, Katrina. I'll talk to the others. We'll find a way to keep you safe."

She opened her arms and Jacob obliged. It was the first time he'd ever hugged his cousin.

* * * * *

That night, after all the Laudners had gone to bed, Jacob was pleasantly surprised to be awakened by Malini crawling through his window. He helped her the rest of the way, then took her in his arms, lifting her from the floor and spinning her around toward the bed. She giggled softly into his ear as he laid her down gently and crawled in beside her.

"We need to talk," she said.

Jacob's stomach twisted. She was a Healer now. The medicine woman was capable of seeing the future. Did she already know about Mara? Did she know about the kiss?

"I wanted to tell you, Malini. I was just waiting for the right time."

"Tell me what?"

"About what happened with Mara. Isn't that what you wanted to talk to me about?"

Malini sat up in bed, pulling away from him. Her eyes grew wide and glowed golden in the dark room, like a cat's. "Actually, I wanted to talk to you about what I thought you could do to win over my father. But now I'm much more interested in what you have to tell me about Mara." Her voice was clipped.

Jacob sat on the side of the bed. He rubbed his eyes and wished he'd kept his mouth shut. But then again, he'd wanted to tell her since the moment it happened. It was eating him up inside.

"She kissed me," he blurted. He looked across the room at his desk. If he met her eyes he'd never be able to finish. "And I guess I kissed her back before I knew what was happening."

All the air seemed to rush from the room. Jacob heard a small intake of breath behind him, but Malini didn't say anything. "It didn't mean anything. We were sparring and she initiated it. I stopped it as soon as I knew what was happening."

This time Malini did say something. "Look me in the eye and tell me you're not attracted to her."

Jacob turned and met Malini's new golden stare. There was a time that, when he looked at her, all he saw was soft warmth. Now her eyes were hard and powerful. "I don't love her, Malini. I love you."

"That's not what I asked." She stood and walked to the window.

He followed her, placing his hands on her shoulders and whispering into her ear. "So what? It's stupid. I'm not going to lie to you and say I wasn't, but it doesn't matter. I'm attracted to *you* and I love *you*. We are meant to be together." He held his right hand in front of her face and twirled the ring she'd given him for Christmas with his thumb. It was engraved with the word "Water" in Sanskrit. She'd told him it was her destiny. *He* was her destiny.

She cleared her throat and turned to face him. He was surprised her eyes were dry. He'd thought she was crying when she walked to the window.

"When I went through the stone, I told you that Death gave me this hand, but I didn't tell you how. He kissed me."

"Death ... kissed you." Jacob reflexively took a step back from her. He didn't mean to, but there was so much he didn't understand about her journey.

"Yes. I felt the icy chill of the grave. I saw in my mind the horrors of war, of plague, of hunger ... the things he sees every day. We danced together. He made this for me." She moved the neck of her shirt aside and he saw the medicine woman's stone mounted in gold and diamonds around her neck.

"What are you saying, Malini? Are you breaking up with me to be with Death?"

"No, Jacob. I'm saying that when you've only kissed one person, it's exciting when another person kisses you. I was attracted to Death. I admit it. You were attracted to Mara. I knew you were the moment she stepped through the portal. She's beautiful and strong and it's only natural you would be."

"So we're even. We can put this behind us." Jacob exhaled a breath he didn't even know he was holding.

"There's something more I need to tell you." Malini rubbed her hands together between them. "I found out that water heals me. When I use my power, my body burns. You saw the way my skin blistered when I healed Katrina. Water cures me. Any water. The message the Buddhist monk gave me when I was six, it wasn't about you at all. It was about me. I was wrong when I told you that you were my destiny."

Jacob stopped, breathless. He took a few steps back and sat down on the bed. "What are you saying?"

"I'm saying we're just two teenagers who like each other, nothing more. Maybe we should take a break. Maybe this is a sign we aren't supposed to be together."

"No. We can get beyond this." Jacob tried to swallow, but his throat had constricted and his eyes burned.

"Get beyond this? I don't want to have to get beyond anything. Listen, either we're meant to be or we're not. And right now, Jacob, if you're kissing another girl while I'm fighting for my life, we are so not."

What had he been thinking? All this time he thought once everything was out in the open, she would forgive him. He'd thought they were indestructible.

He couldn't answer her. He just nodded. That short movement of his head was the most difficult physical activity he'd ever challenged himself with.

"It's settled then," she said. Her voice broke a little. She opened the window and didn't wait for Jacob to help her out. She was down the rose lattice and to her staff before he reached the opening.

Just before she tapped the staff, he saw that she was sobbing. He held up his hand to stop her. Maybe there was a chance she was having second thoughts and hope that he could set things right. But she was already gone.

Chapter 25
Freedom

"You've got to be kidding me?" Dane dropped his fork on his orange tray and looked skeptically at Malini and Jacob. "You guys really broke up. Three weeks before prom, who knows how long before the Watcher apocalypse, and you guys decide to break up. Yeah, that makes a shitload of sense."

"Drop it, Dane," Jacob said.

Dane leaned back in his chair. "Whatever. Tell me what's going on then. What do I need to know?"

Jacob was thankful for the change in subject. "Katrina went back to school. Gideon went with her for protection. He's the only one that can completely conceal himself if he needs to, plus be back here in the blink of an eye when the Watchers come."

"That brings up a good point. Why aren't they here? What are they waiting for?

"Dr. Silva says she thinks they are readying themselves. Time moves faster here than there. When I was in Nod, I thought I was only there for a few hours but three days had passed. If they are organizing themselves, it may just be a matter of timing."

"I think it's more than that," Malini said. She rubbed her right forearm like it was sore. "I think they're waiting for something. Watchers are opportunists. They're lazy. Something is going to happen that makes it easier for them to get the best of us."

Dane locked eyes with her. "I thought you could, like, see the future now. Don't you know what's coming?"

Malini twisted her hair between her fingers. "That's not my gift. The medicine woman could see the future. I'm life and death, remember?" She toyed with the stone around her neck. "Maybe I could ask her. I haven't been through since I got back. She might be able to help us."

Jacob grunted. "Um, yeah, that might be a good idea. I mean, it's just our lives hanging in the balance here. We had enough trouble polishing off two of them in Chicago. It might be nice to know if thirty of them are going to storm Paris next week."

"Hey! I'm new at this. You don't have to be such a bastard about it. Why don't you worry about you? Go spar with Mara and get off my case."

Dane stood and lifted his orange tray, even though there was fifteen minutes left for lunch. "Thank you, you two. Glad to know my life is in the hands of two people who obviously love each other but are too proud to admit it." He strolled away toward the conveyor belt, leaving Jacob and Malini seething in opposite directions at their regular table.

* * * * *

After school, Malini walked into her room and slammed the door. Oooh, Jacob made her so angry. To be the one who kissed another girl and then to act all hurt around Dane about breaking up. It was a joke. And now he was being critical of her new responsibilities as a Healer. Well, he could just shove it.

She tossed her backpack on the side of her desk and flopped down on her bed. Her room seemed to taunt her. Everywhere there were pictures of places she wanted to go: the Eiffel Tower, a safari in Kenya, the Grand Canyon. She had always wanted to be a citizen of the world, to help people. But she never wanted this.

From the time she was small, she'd wanted to be a journalist. If she was someone who had access to the events of the world, she could shed light on corruption, and bring help to those who were hopeless by telling their story. That's how she wanted to help. Now, as a Healer, she was expected to dole out life and death. She was like a human version of the scales of justice. Who wanted that kind of responsibility? It was so unfair.

A knock on her door made her jump. "Come in!" she called.

The door creaked open and her father walked in. He stood awkwardly in the center of her room.

"How was your day?" he asked.

"Fine."

"You don't seem fine."

"I'm fine."

"You seem upset. Maybe if you talk to me about it, it will help."

Malini crossed her arms over her chest and looked out the window. "Dad, no offense, but you don't have any idea what I'm going through. There is no way talking to you about this is going to help."

Her father folded his hands behind his back and raised his chin. He walked to the window. Looking out over the side yard, he placed himself in her line of sight.

"Maybe not. When I was your age, I wasn't allowed the freedoms you have. We were taught to concentrate on our studies. I used to sneak out to see your mother. It was years before my parents knew about her and then my father was furious." His voice trailed off. He seemed distracted.

"You snuck out to see Mom? What, in India?"

"Yes, India. Your mother was in a different caste than my family. It wasn't customary for us to court each other."

"But you did."

He smiled a slow, broad grin. "I did. I married her anyway. I'd say we've made our own traditions."

Even though her mom had told her the history before, this was more personal information than her father had ever shared with her. The sudden confession made her suspicious. "Dad, what is this about?"

"I realized something today, Malini. In just a couple of months, you are going to be seventeen years old."

Malini sat up in bed, crossing her legs in front of her. "You just realized how old I was?"

"In less than a year and a half, you'll go away to college."

"Um, yeah. I guess." Malini wondered how college would fit in with her new responsibilities.

"I grounded you for the last five months to keep you safe and you were almost killed by a random act of violence. Now we're talking about moving, about selling the business to keep you safe."

"I told you before, I don't think that's necessary—" He cut her off with a wave of his hand.

"You know what I think? I think, I won't ever succeed at keeping you safe, Malini. Because at almost seventeen you're not supposed to be safe. When I was your age, I was taking risks with my life, with my family, and most importantly, with my heart." He turned toward her. The light behind his head from the window made it impossible to see the details of his face.

"What are you saying, Dad?"

"I'm saying, you're not grounded anymore. I'm saying you can go to prom with whomever you want to, whether I like them or not. I'm saying that we're not moving. Live your life, Malini." His hand motioned around the room, toward all of the pictures of all of the worldly places. "Do what it is you want to do! Do the thing that will make you happy! I did and I have never regretted it."

He stopped talking. Malini flew from the bed and wrapped her arms around her father. She kissed his cheek and hugged him as tightly as she could.

"I love you, Daddy," she said.

"I love you, too."

"I broke up with Jacob. That's why I'm upset. I thought we were destined for each other but I guess not."

Her father looked down into her face, stroking her hair back from her eyes with his hand. "Don't you know about destiny, Malini? Destiny is not a place that we navigate to like a pinpoint on a map. Destiny is a fabric woven from our choices. It is the cloak we wear every day and the shroud that covers us in our death. You can't wait for destiny to find you. You make it for yourself."

Malini tossed the words around in her head. Destiny is a fabric woven from our choices. She thought about the sari she'd worn on the other side, made out of the experiences of her ancestors. In a way, all of their choices had helped her. All of their lives had created who she was and given her guidance when she needed it most.

"Thank you," she said through happy tears. "Thank you for trusting me."

He kissed her forehead and headed for the door. She could clearly see the wet gloss in his eyes now, the tears hanging on his lashes. "Mom says dinner in a half-hour."

"Okay."

He closed the door behind him.

More than anything, at that moment, Malini felt blessed. And somehow, with that knowledge firmly in her heart, she was able to do what she was meant to do. Quietly, she locked her bedroom door.

She hooked her fingers around the gold chain at her neck and pulled the red stone pendent over her head. Leaning back against the pillows on her bed, she focused on the stone as it dangled in the afternoon light. The transition to the other side was quick, as if her body had become used to the idea.

Fatima was at her loom, the *woosh-woosh* of the shuttle creating a peaceful rhythm. "Welcome back, Malini."

"Fatima, I need help. I need to know when the Watchers are coming."

"You know better than to ask me. I don't know the future. Only the past and the pattern it creates."

"But patterns repeat themselves in the cloth. What does the pattern tell you about what could happen?"

She gave a husky laugh. "I would say that sometime between now and a hundred years from now, the Watchers will try to kill you. You are this generation's Noah. You are the leader. They wish to bring about a new flood and you are humanity's best hope for stopping them."

"Sometime between now and a hundred years from now. Great. I don't suppose you can be more specific."

Fatima held up a length of cloth. "This tapestry is the history of every person in your world over the last fifteen seconds. Each stitch is a choice. You tell me if you could be more specific."

Malini looked at the yards of fabric shimmering in Fatima's arms. "Point made," she said. "I need to consult with the medicine woman. Can you tell me how to reach her?"

"You're in luck. She's on the veranda having tea with Death." She motioned toward the archway.

Malini walked out into the daylight glow. The tiny Peruvian woman was hunched at the table across from Death. He sat unnaturally straight on the teak patio furniture watching Wisnu chase something small, brown, and furry through the yard.

"May I join you?" Malini said.

They both turned at once. "Of course!" the medicine woman said. "We've been waiting for you."

Death smiled, but lowered his eyes when she looked in his direction. He stood in the same stiff fashion as he sat, straightening his tuxedo and pulling out her chair for her with a gentlemanly bow. She sat down as he pushed it back in.

"I need to know when the Watchers will come," she said.

"And what makes you think that I know better than you?" she said. Malini could tell she wasn't speaking English but somehow she could understand exactly what she was saying.

"I thought you could see the future? I thought that's why you gave the stone to Jacob? He said he used it to find out what would happen."

"It is true that I can see possible futures, but you are capable of the same. It's part of being a Healer."

"How? How do I see it?"

"This sari shop—this is your vision space. When Jacob comes here, it is a hardware store. When I come here in my own power, it is a garden of Manioc root. When I want to see the possible futures, I pick up a handful of earth and let it drift through my fingers. The answer comes in the individual grains of sand. The Earth mother makes the dirt. I read the dirt."

"You mean to say that I should read the threads of the sari material inside? But there are millions of yards of it! How could I possibly find what I'm looking for?"

"That is why I meditate and purify myself. A pure mind sees clearly. It takes practice."

"So you meditate, and that is how you know which dirt to pick up?"

"Yes. And you will know which fabric to pick up. But use it sparingly. Too much prediction can be a self-fulfilling prophecy. In fact, I rarely tell those who ask the whole truth of what I see. It might take away their ability to change it."

Malini sighed and took a sip of the tea Death had poured for her. She noticed his left hand had inched across the table toward her right. The proximity made the bones thrum beneath her glove. Tiny sparks seemed to climb up her spine when she turned to meet his black eyes.

She shook her head and turned back toward the medicine woman. "Can you tell me what you see? This one time, can you help me? I'm still learning."

"I will do what you ask, Malini, but then you must do something for me."

"What? Anything. I'll do anything."

"I want you to come to see me in the physical world, in the Achuar village where I live. I want you to come with the boy who visited me before. What was his name? Jacob. Come with Jacob. And when you come I will ask you to do something and you must do it."

Malini crossed her arms and frowned. "I'm not sure I can make Jacob come. We're not … getting along right now." She felt her shoulders tense and her blood boil at the thought of him.

"Those are my terms."

"Fine. I'll find a way." Jacob wouldn't deny her if it meant stopping the Watchers.

"Henry, would you leave us? This is a future that is only Malini's to know."

Death stood and gave a small bow.

"You have a name? Like a real name?" Malini blurted at Death.

"Of course. I was human once, just like you. My name is Henry." He reached out as if to shake her hand but when she extended hers he lifted it between his fingers and kissed the back of it instead. He turned as if to go.

On impulse Malini stood, knocking over her chair.

"Henry, would you like to go to the prom with me?"

His dark eyes burned, growing wider at the question. "Of course. I would adore the chance."

"Great! It's—"

"Oh, I know. I know exactly when it is." With another small bow and a turn of his shaggy brown head, he took three steps into the yard and disappeared entirely.

It took a moment for Malini to realize the medicine woman was laughing next to her. "What's so funny?"

"It's a brave young woman indeed that invites death into her life."

"You mean that figuratively, right? I mean, he seems like such a nice guy and kind of, I don't know, lonely."

"I wonder why that is?" She cleared her throat. "But to the task at hand." The old woman braced herself on the corner of the table and reached one arthritic hand to the ground. She scooped up a fistful of dirt and let it cascade through her fingers. "I see the streets of Paris flooded with angels and Watchers. Soon ... when the Earth is just waking up and the crops are saplings."

"Will we survive?'

She squinted at the dirt. "One among you has the power to save all of you at a great price. You must trust in those around you to do the right thing, even when you are not sure what the right thing is."

"What does that mean?"

The medicine woman opened her eyes. "That is all I see." She poked Malini's shoulder. "Now you come. You come as you have promised."

Malini rested her chin in her hand, feeling swindled. At least she knew they were coming before summer. "Yeah. Okay," she said.

"One more thing," The old woman stopped at the archway. Malini noticed the painful way she bent forward and wondered how it felt to carry the weight of over two hundred years. "You don't need the stone anymore to come here. This place is inside of you. You can come here anytime you want. Give the stone away to another you think needs access to this place."

"Thank you."

"And don't forget to come see me." She looked in the direction of Death's castle and sighed deeply. "I think it's best you come before prom."

"I promise," Malini said.

The woman took two steps and vanished. Malini stood and walked into the shop, overwhelmed by the bolts of fabric that were stacked floor to ceiling. Would she ever be able to read them the way the medicine woman read the dirt? It was too much for her to take in. She said her goodbyes to Fatima, and returned to her room on the other side.

Chapter 26
Visitor

In the dark of his room, Jacob opened his eyes, tensing with the intuition that he was not alone. He tried to even out his breathing beneath the covers, to feign sleep a few minutes longer while he sifted through the sounds. There was someone shifting near his desk. Whoever it was took a seat in the chair.

"I know you're awake, Jacob." Mara's whisper coasted across the room.

Jacob sat up in bed, letting the comforter fall around his waist. It took a moment for him to remember he wasn't wearing a shirt. He yanked the sheet up to his neck. "Mara, what are doing here?" He looked toward the window. "How did you get in? I know I locked that window."

Mara reached toward her feet and lifted a staff from the floor. "Dr. Silva's. No one hears anything when time stops." She grinned sheepishly. "I couldn't sleep."

Well that explained it. Jacob rolled to the side of the bed, taking the sheet with him, and grabbed a T-shirt off the floor. He noticed it didn't smell great as he pulled it over his head, but hey, he wasn't expecting company. Once he was dressed, he sat on the side of his bed and spread his hands. "So, are you here to make sure both of us are equally exhausted when we practice tomorrow or is something on your mind?"

She twisted the chair on its base. "I want to apologize. What happened with Malini ... I never meant to break you guys up. This is my fault. I started it. I can talk to her if you want. Maybe if I explain things—"

"How do you know? We just broke up last night."

"It's a small town, Jacob."

"Yeah, but you never leave Dr. Silva's house!"

"Okay. Umm, Dr. Silva told me. She heard from Mrs. Westcott at the grocery store."

"Great. I hate Paris."

"Anyway, I just came to apologize and to offer to talk to her for you." She picked at her thumbnail absently.

"It wasn't your fault. She kissed someone else, too."

"What?"

"Yeah. Death. Apparently the hand was some kind of make-out gift."

"You're kidding." Mara perked up in her chair.

"I wish I was. And she seemed only too ready to be done with me. You know, I thought we had something. I thought it was…" Jacob's hands tightened into fists. "Fate. I thought it was fate."

"And she broke up with you?"

"Yes. And now she's acting all pissed at me all the time."

"Hmm." Mara sat back in her chair and crossed her legs. Jacob noticed she was wearing a skirt and strappy sandals.

"Hey, I thought you said you couldn't sleep?"

"I couldn't."

"Why are you all dressed up?"

Mara took a deep breath. "I couldn't very well let you see me in my pajamas." She giggled nervously.

Jacob grinned. Mara never giggled. He knew she liked him and there was no getting around that he was attracted to her but … but … He'd run out of excuses. There was no reason he couldn't pursue a relationship with Mara. If he wanted to, he could kiss her right now. But that was the problem, he didn't know if he wanted to.

The silence surrounded them like a heavy shroud. Time stretched on awkwardly from the giggle. It was his turn to say something. He searched his brain for something to say.

"Sooo, it wasn't your fault. Don't feel guilty. You didn't do anything wrong." He rubbed his palms on his thighs.

In a flash, she was sitting next to him on the bed. He couldn't tell if she had stopped time or if she'd just moved quickly. All Soulkeepers were faster than regular humans and he was definitely distracted. His desk chair spun on its swivel.

She leaned forward. He could smell her perfume. Malini never wore perfume. She always smelled clean, like soap. Jacob wondered what kind of perfume it was. The closer she got the more it seemed to suffocate him, like he was burying his face in a bouquet of lilies at the shop, too sweet, too floral.

Before her lips could hit his, he stood and crossed the room. He wasn't sure why he'd dodged the kiss. But until he sorted out his feelings, he had to say something to put her off.

"Would you go to the prom with me, Mara? I mean, you're stuck here anyway until we figure this Watcher threat out. You might as well have some fun while you're here."

"Yeah! Shit, yeah. That would be great."

"Good. It's a date. Um, maybe we should have a date before we do anything else. You know, get to know each other first."

Mara looked disappointed but walked to the staff and lifted it from the floor. "Yeah. That's a good idea. Two weeks from Saturday, right?"

"Right.'"

"I'm looking forward to it."

"Me, too."

"Goodbye, Jacob."

"See ya." Jacob watched as she raised her bell and vanished. He had the oddest feeling that Mara hadn't left immediately after she'd stopped time. Her perfume smelled stronger than it had a moment before and there was a wetness on his lips. He ran the back of his hand across his mouth. It came away red.

Lipstick.

Chapter 27
The Promise

"Wait for it …Wait for it …" Malini whispered to herself from behind the bank of lockers. She'd promised the medicine woman she'd visit before prom and had effectively procrastinated as long as conceivably possible. Now she had only a week and a half to keep her promise. She was waiting for Jacob to enter his combination and open his locker. With his hands busily swapping out books he was less likely to avoid her.

Malini stepped up behind him. "Jacob, I need to talk to you."

He jerked upward, banging his head on the shelf. "Damn!" He grabbed his head and turned to face her. "Jeez, Malini. Do you mind?"

"I need to talk to you."

"About what?"

"There's something we need to do before prom."

Jacob's face paled and he took a step back from her. "I thought we weren't going to prom anymore. You broke up with me, remember?"

"There's something we have to do before the date of prom. Of course we aren't going to prom ... I mean not together."

"Right, because I'm already going with someone else."

"Let me guess. Mara." There was too much venom in the way she said her name. She didn't want Jacob to think she was jealous. That was just ridiculous considering she was going to prom with Henry.

"Yes, Mara. I see no reason why I shouldn't have asked her. I didn't want to go alone."

"There is no reason. I'm sure you two will have a fabulous time. I'm going, too, by the way."

"With who?" Now it was Jacob's voice that held the edge.

"Stop. This isn't what I came here to talk to you about and we only have a few minutes before class." Already, the hall was emptying. She needed to get him to agree, now.

"Then spill it."

"We need to go see the medicine woman."

"I thought *you* were the medicine woman."

"When I was on the other side, I promised I would take you to see her before prom. There's something she needs us to do."

"Why me?"

"She didn't say. But she made me swear. I know she wouldn't if it wasn't important."

"Fine. Saturday. Meet in the forest behind Dr. Silva's. We'll use the staffs. Hopefully, it won't take long." He pulled a stack of books into his arms and slammed the locker—hard.

"Oh, believe me, I'll be doing everything in my power to make it as short a trip as possible," she said, but she wasn't sure he heard her. He was halfway down the hall and the bell was ringing. Malini forced herself to turn away and headed for class.

* * * * *

No matter how much time Malini spent dreading Saturday, it came anyway. She drove to Dr. Silva's, anxious to get the trip over with. Every minute she was with Jacob was another minute of feeling like her still-beating heart was being torn from her chest.

She parked her car, grabbed her staff out of the trunk, and hurried toward the woods. With so much to do before prom, she hoped this wouldn't take long. She needed to find a dress to wear. Shopping was impossible. What did you wear to a dance with Death? The red dress she'd worn during her initiation was perfect, but she'd never find anything like that in the human world. What was she thinking inviting an immortal to prom, anyway? No one could live up to the expectations of prom night, let alone the added stress of being someone's first date in who knows how many millennia.

"It's about time. I've been waiting for like fifteen minutes." Jacob was standing at the edge of the woods with his staff in hand.

"I thought we said noon? It's only twelve-oh-five."

"Well, I assumed when you said noon you wanted to be there by noon. I allowed for travel time."

"That's the stupidest thing I've ever heard. We have enchanted staffs. It takes like two seconds to go anywhere. Besides, we're going to the Achuar village. They don't even own a clock. It's not like we can be late."

"Fine. Let's just go." He held out his hand to her.

"What's that for?"

"We need to hold hands so that we end up in the same place at the same time."

"Why can't we just both pop over to the village?"

"Do you even know how to get there? Have you been there before?"

Malini thought about that one. She'd only met the medicine woman *in between,* as Fatima called it. She hadn't actually been to her village. For the staffs to work, she needed to picture where she was going clearly.

"Point made," she said and slipped her hand into his. As soon as she did, she regretted it. Her mouth went dry and a zing of electricity traveled through her. Their eyes met. More than anything she wanted him to kiss her. She hated herself for it but she did. He leaned forward, stepping into her, and for a moment she thought he felt it to, that he might close the remaining distance between them. But he didn't. He simply squeezed her hand and lifted his staff. With a crack and a flash of light, they were standing in the Achuar village.

The villagers came running, the children grabbing their hands, the adults chattering back and forth between themselves in a language Malini didn't know.

"They're asking each other if we're gods," Jacob said.

"You can understand them?"

"Ever since last year when I was here, I've been able to speak other languages. Remember in Nod, how I could read the signs? I guess it's part of my gift."

"But I was there in the parking lot. Your gift was … is the ability to manipulate water. It's weird that the language thing came on later."

"Our gifts, our powers, develop over time. I don't claim to understand it but it's pretty much saved my Spanish grade this semester."

"Nice. Why don't you go for broke and be a languages major—really milk the gift for all it's worth."

"Good idea."

They turned when they saw the medicine woman emerge from her hut. She said a few words in the language Malini didn't understand.

"She's inviting us in," Jacob said.

Malini followed him into the small thatched roof hut and joined the old woman sitting cross-legged on a woven grass mat.

There was a selection of herbs and oils in front of her. She mashed them together using a stone mortar and pestle. Standing, she dribbled the concoction in a large circle around Jacob and Malini, and then returned to her place within its boundaries.

"For protection and purity," Jacob translated. "What we are about to do is dangerous, but it must be done."

The medicine woman smiled broadly. With only two or three teeth left in her mouth, Malini wondered how she managed on a jungle diet. The old woman said something to Jacob in her native tongue. His face turned bright red. He didn't translate.

Malini poked Jacob's leg emphatically, until he relented and whispered the translation. "Malini, she's offered to bind us together."

"Bind us together? What does that mean?"

"Umm. I … ah … think it's like a ceremony. Like what she does for her tribe."

"You mean, like *marrying* us?"

"She says it's considered an honor for her to offer without being asked. What should I say?"

"You say, 'no,' that's what you say. We're sixteen years old and we're not even going out anymore! It's ridiculous."

Jacob translated, although she was sure his respectful tone did not include the part about it being ridiculous.

The medicine woman nodded slowly, her gap-toothed smile melting a little. She said something that sounded almost like she was chiding Jacob.

"What did she say?" Malini asked.

"That one was meant for me." He looked down at the dirt.

The old woman reached for Malini's right hand, the hand of Death, and pointed at the crook of her elbow. She said a few words and her face grew positively grim.

Jacob's head snapped up, his attention turning to Malini's hand. He cleared his throat before translating. "She says it's her time. She wants you to release her. I think she wants you to kill her."

Malini yanked her hand back. "*No!*"

The medicine woman sat back on her heels, her face serene. She folded her hands in front of her chest, as if in prayer, bowing her head in Malini's direction, and spoke to her in a pleading tone.

Jacob translated. "It's the only way she can die. The next Healer must release the first or she will live forever. She has lived for two-hundred-fifty-eight years waiting for you. Living is very painful for her and she begs for your mercy." Jacob's voice cracked.

"I don't think I can do it. I'm not a murderer. It's too awful."

"I think you have to do it, Malini. She's suffering. Look at her. What if this was you? What if you were forced to serve as a Soulkeeper for over two centuries and the only way you could die is if the next Healer let you go? You need to help her."

"I'll heal her. Tell her I'll heal her."

Jacob translated. The medicine woman responded, sounding absolutely furious.

"She doesn't want to be healed. She's outlived her husband and children. She's watched countless villagers die. She says it's her time. She wants to die."

"I can't. I can't murder someone."

Jacob scooped her left hand into his. "It wouldn't be murder, Malini; it would be mercy."

Malini remembered what Death had said, that the world thought of him as a curse when in fact he was also a blessing. The medicine woman hunched in front of her, her dress exposing the bones of her shoulders. Her father's words came back to her. When they were in Springfield, he'd said Abraham Lincoln was his hero because somehow he knew the Civil War would be worth it. She was a Healer. Part of her job was to look at a situation and know right from wrong. And right wasn't always about life.

If this was how it had always been done, then it was her responsibility to release the medicine woman. The fear, the hesitation she felt, she had to admit it was selfish. She did not want to be alone in the world. If she helped the medicine woman to die, she would be the lone Healer. She wasn't ready. Selfishly, she wanted the medicine woman to live to help her.

The circle of protection made sense now. If Malini did this, a huge target would be painted on her back.

"Ask her what her name is. I will not do it without knowing the name she was given at birth."

Jacob translated and the woman answered in a soft, pleading voice.

"She says, Panctu Soolta."

Malini dug her fingers into the bend of her arm and peeled back the glove of flesh from her bones. The hand glowed pale in the shade of the hut. The medicine woman's eyes flared at the sight of it. She lowered herself onto her side within the circle. She mumbled something into the dirt.

"She says, thank you and to hurry, please. I think she wants to get it over with." Jacob reached over and squeezed Malini's left hand. "It's okay. Do it."

Malini lowered her right hand toward the medicine woman's shoulder. The deadly skeletal fingers hovered just over the skin but she couldn't force herself to touch the woman.

Henry walked through the wall of the hut and to Panctu's side. He smiled at Malini before bowing to Panctu.

"Who is that?"

"Henry. I mean Death. He's come for her soul."

Henry's eyes had turned from black to the burning caverns she'd seen in the ballroom. "It's time, Malini. It won't hurt. I'll take care of her," he said.

Malini lowered her hand onto the woman. The feeling was not unpleasant but was as unsettling as any she'd encountered. Her fingers met skin and the woman's body convulsed. In seconds, the movement stopped. Death reached forward, but his hand did not stop at Panctu's skin. His fingers slid into her flesh as easily as if she were made of water. He hooked his fingers on something and tugged.

Panctu's translucent form rose from her body as if she were hatching from a cocoon. And her ghost was young! Her hair was sleek black, her skin smooth, and she stood straight and strong at Death's side smiling a full set of teeth. The thing that he had hooked with his fingers was her soul.

Death led Panctu from the circle. A door appeared in the hut, a thatched door that might have been the entrance to a Hawaiian-themed room at a five star resort. Henry reached forward and turned the knob. The light that poured out when it opened was so bright Malini had to turn away. When he closed the door again, plunging the hut back into shadow, Panctu was gone.

Malini slid her hand back into the glove, then wiped the tears that were cascading Niagara Falls style down her face. She looked toward Henry, who had the smallest of smiles.

"See you Saturday," he said and then he was gone.

Jacob jerked by her side. "Oh my God, Malini, does that mean you're going to die on Saturday?" His arms wrapped around her in an attempt at comfort but he was nearing hysterics, babbling on about what he would do to fight off Death.

"No—" Malini unwrapped herself from his arms and grabbed his hands in demand of his full attention. "He's my prom date. He was talking about prom."

Jacob's jaw dropped open and he pulled away from her. "You invited THAT to prom?"

"He has a name, Jacob. He used to be human once. His name is Henry and he gave me this. Remember?" She held up her right hand, the hand she had used to kill.

"Right. The kiss. Wow." Jacob stood, eyes darting away from her. "Just … wow." He stepped out of the circle, grabbed his staff from the wall and exited the hut without looking back.

Chapter 28
Prom

There was no way to prepare for this. Malini flipped through the rack of dresses one by one. Her mother had long since given up on helping her and was sitting on an overstuffed chair outside the fitting room texting someone on her cell phone. She'd offered to take Malini to another store. There was a bridal shop that sold high-end prom attire in Indiana, about forty-five minutes away. But Malini would hate herself for wasting her parents' time and money on a dress she would only wear once. What color did you wear to have your heart broken? She was sure as soon as she saw Jacob with Mara, that's exactly what would happen.

She pulled a red strapless gown from the clearance rack. At least this would match the red stone necklace. Panctu had said it wasn't necessary anymore, but she wasn't ready to give it away, not until she knew for sure that she could cross to the other side without it. Besides, at this point, who needed it more than she did?

Inside the dressing room, she slid into the red sheath dress. There was a slit up the side to her upper thigh adorned with a pattern of rhinestones. She turned to the side, happy that the dress was tight enough through the torso that it wouldn't fall down if she decided to dance. Piling her hair on top of her head, she turned side to side. It wasn't nearly as sexy as the one death had made for her, but more modern and only eighty-nine dollars, which was a major bonus. It would do. Plus she had a pair of black strappy sandals that would go. No need to buy shoes.

She brought the dress out to her mother, who was giggling to herself, staring down at her phone. Her head bobbed up when she noticed Malini. "Your cousin, Ashoke, is getting married. His parents are alarmed because it is a love match and not arranged. It makes me laugh. Wait until they see that the boy you are dating is not even Indian. It will be the day I married your father all over again." She beamed in Malini's direction.

"Mom, I'm not actually dating Jacob anymore. I'm not actually dating anyone."

Her mother's eyebrows knit together. "How did I not know this? When did this happen?"

"We broke up a couple of weeks ago." Malini pressed her lips together.

"Who are you going to prom with then?"

Malini had to think of what to say. "His name is Henry. He's just a friend."

Her mother stood and reached for the hanger of the dress draped across Malini's arm. She looked disturbed, almost angry, as she held it up and pinched the fabric. "I will tell you this, Malini; Jacob Lau will rue the day he broke up with you when he sees you in this. You will make him cry."

She was going to say that she didn't want to make Jacob cry but her mother had already jetted toward the cashier. Deep within her heart, some part of Malini hoped her mother was right.

* * * * *

Malini spent the week staring out windows. What were the Watchers waiting for? She knew it was just a matter of time before an army of fallen angels came for her. She'd expected it would be sooner rather than later. She almost wished it would happen now. That would save her from prom.

She pulled on the red dress and strapped on her black heels. Her hair was curled and piled atop her head. Her makeup was more natural than what she'd worn to dance with Death the first time, but more her style. As a final touch, she reached for the red stone necklace on her bureau.

"Here, let me get that for you." Her mother walked into her room and accepted the gold chain from Malini's hand.

"You look smashing. I might have to hold your date up when he sees you. And that Jacob—"

"Mom, it's okay. I don't want Jacob to suffer for what happened."

Her mother pursed her lips and clipped the stone around her neck. "This necklace is quite lovely." She took the stone in her hand and rubbed her thumb over it. Malini placed her own hand over the jewel on her chest, worried her mother would get pulled across to the other side.

"It's nothing. Cheap costume jewelry I picked up at Macy's the last time we were there."

"I don't remember."

"You were looking at something with dad."

"Oh. Lucky, it matches the dress so well. I think it is a sign you will have the time of your life tonight."

"I hope so." Malini smiled at her mother's enthusiasm just as the sound of the doorbell ringing turned their heads.

"Showtime," her mother said, jogging down the stairs. Malini followed but at a much slower pace; she wasn't used to walking in high heels.

The door was already open by the time she clopped across the marble foyer. Her mother and father turned to her with astonished faces. She shuffled faster to get a view of what was on the other side.

When Death went to prom, he did it up right. Henry stood on her porch looking even more dapper than before. The tuxedo he wore maintained its otherworldly quality, draping majestically over his obviously athletic physique.

Despite his dark sunglasses, she knew he was checking her out. Besides the flare of red she caught behind the shades, the corner of his mouth lifted.

It was what she saw behind him in her driveway that had left her parents speechless. There was a carriage, black and intricately carved like something out of Victorian England, being pulled by two sleek black horses that were neighing and hoofing the pavement. The sun was setting behind this scene, painting the sky red and purple. All she could think of was how the picture outside her door belonged in a movie scene, not in her life, not in anyone's real life.

"It has been a sincere pleasure to meet you, Mr. and Mrs. Gupta," Henry said in a soft voice that commanded more attention than its volume let on. He extended his hand toward her. "Shall we go? Your awesome beauty will have me standing in the doorway for hours if I'm not careful." The compliment made the bones of her right hand vibrate, as if he'd plucked a cord that thrummed through her body.

She placed the tingling hand in his and that part of her went home. She allowed Henry to lead her out the door. Her father scurried to find his camera. He snapped a half-dozen pictures of them in the yard and then another dozen getting into the carriage.

When the door was finally closed and her father had lowered the camera, the driver turned back and tipped his hat in her direction. Malini saw a flash of bones through the illusion of his flesh. With a crack of the reins, the horses broke into an even trot and Malini waved goodbye to her parents.

"This is amazing, Henry," she said.

"It is not every day I get to have a truly human experience. It's been decades since I've been invited here and normally my visits are on the heels of tragedy."

"You said you used to be human?"

"Oh, yes. I was your age when I was chosen," he said sadly. Malini got the sense that it was a distressing memory and didn't press him with questions.

"I think you'll enjoy yourself tonight. Our friend, Dane, has helped plan the entire event. There's a dinner and dancing. It should be fun."

He turned toward her, orangey flames licking up around her reflection in his pupils. "I enjoy dancing with you, Malini. You are the first in over a century to make me think about beginnings. My world is usually about endings."

"Do you think it's because of the hand? It vibrates a little when I'm near you."

"It is highly possible. Your hand is a piece of me. I've never given a gift of that magnitude before."

Malini leaned back in the seat and tossed the comment around in her head. It was odd to think of having a piece of someone attached to your body. Frankenstein-ish. If she hadn't been a freak before, this certainly pushed her over the edge. She couldn't meet his eyes, so she looked out toward the driver and the horses. A ray of light from the sunset broke through the clouds and she could see his bones x-ray style.

"The driver is dead." It wasn't a question.

"Yes. As are the horses. Besides you and the immortals, all of my friends are dead."

Malini smoothed her dress as they pulled into the parking lot of Paris High School. "Maybe it would be best if the other students didn't know who you were. Can we just say you're from a school up north?"

"Agreed. And don't worry, the only reason you can tell about the driver and the horses is your hand. To humans they appear quite alive."

"That's a relief."

The carriage came to a halt. The driver jumped down from his bench and swung open the door, reaching for her hand to help her down. At first she offered her left, but the man snatched his away before she could touch him.

"Not your healing hand, Malini. Sam is perfectly happy with remaining dead."

She offered her right and gingerly stepped down to the pavement. There were hoards of students arriving and they were all staring. A couple of the wealthier students had rented limos but no one had procured a horse-drawn carriage. As far as Malini knew, this was a first for Paris. But the carriage wasn't the only reason the other students were snapping pictures, some more candidly than others.

"Henry, has anyone ever told you, you look remarkably like a certain pop star?"

"What's a pop star?"

"Pop is a type of music. Popular stuff. You look like a certain popular musician."

"Like Mozart? I look like a modern-day Mozart?"

"I was actually thinking more like a modern-day Bieber."

"Bieber? Never heard of him."

"You could be brothers." A bigger, darker, and more sophisticated brother.

"I hope he's a respectable musician then. I would hate our resemblance to sully your friends' first impression of me."

"Oh, he's respectable. There will be no sullying," Malini said. If anything there might be jealousy, and she was hoping that one boy in particular would suffer from the green monster.

He took her elbow and led her toward the double doors in a straight-backed gesture that belonged somewhere in the past or in a fairy tale but not in Paris, Illinois. There were people attending in jeans and sport jackets. Malini was certain that no one would suspect that Henry was Death, but the way he looked, everyone would know he wasn't from Paris.

Henry held the door for her and she walked to a welcome table surrounded by students. When the crowd broke, she saw Dane handing out favors.

"Malini! Happy prom. Here's your table card. Would you like halo or wings?"

"What?"

"The theme … Haven't you noticed? It's heaven on Earth."

Malini took a good look around. Cut-out clouds hung from the ceiling, puffy cotton mounds filled the corners and the signs were decorated in sparkly gold. The doors to the gym were painted to look like the pearly gates.

"Wow ...this is..."

"Heavenly?" He held up a headband with a tinsel halo and a set of feathery white wings with elastic straps. "They hook on your shoulders. I have them in black, too."

"I'll take a halo," Malini said. Henry reached for a pair of black wings.

"What happened to your zombie idea?"

Malini turned at the sound of Jacob's voice behind her. He was dressed in a black tux with a gray cummerbund that matched the color of Mara's filmy spaghetti-strap dress. She realized she was staring but couldn't stop herself.

"If either of you would have attended any of the prom planning meetings, you would know that the zombie idea was shot down. Not romantic enough. This little stroke of genius was also my idea however. I feel vindicated." Dane handed Jacob and Mara wings, pausing once he noticed the stare-fest between Malini and Jacob.

"You look beautiful, Malini," Jacob said. His eyes washed over her, then settled on Henry. His lids lowered to a more menacing glare. "I don't believe we've officially met. I'm Jacob." He extended his hand in Henry's direction.

Henry shook the hand offered to him and bowed slightly at the waist. "I'm Henry," he said. "Malini's date." Malini knew when Jacob noticed Henry's inhuman gaze. He jumped backward a little, dropping Henry's hand like it was hot.

Mara scowled, embarrassed by the rude gesture, and took up Henry's hand. "I'm Mara. It's nice to meet you, Henry."

Henry met her eyes as he had Jacob's but she didn't jerk when she noticed what he was. Instead, she sank into his stare with a sort of open-mouthed enthrallment that Malini found slightly unsettling.

"You all should go inside," Dane interrupted, clearing his throat. "They're going to serve dinner soon. It's chicken. Everyone loves chicken."

All four of them turned to look at Dane. After an awkward pause, Malini remembered her manners. "Will you be joining us at our table, Dane?"

"You bet. I'll see ya in there." Dane turned to greet Phillip Westcott, who was attending with Amy Barger. Malini's stomach dropped. She thought of how hard this must be for Dane. She made a silent promise to try to help him have a good time tonight and gave him a reassuring nod.

Taking Henry's hand, she led him through the pearly gates. Inside the gym, Malini wove her way to table eight, taking in the dance floor and the D.J., who was looking bored in the corner. The walls were decorated with black material and peppered with stars. A shiny moon crescent dangled from the ceiling along with more clouds and stars.

"This doesn't look anything like Heaven, Malini," Henry said. He scowled at the celestial decorations.

Mara, who'd followed them to the table, grabbed his elbow. "You've been to Heaven?"

"Not exactly. I've seen what it looks like through the door—"

"Henry!" Malini snapped. She lowered her voice to a harsh whisper. "Remember what we talked about. You're a normal teenage boy from a different school."

"Is she not a Soulkeeper?" he whispered back.

"Yes, but there are ears everywhere. This is not the time."

Mara crossed her arms across the front of her dress and glowered at Malini. "Oh, please." She waved her hand around the room. "Look at these people. They're so into themselves. No one gives a damn what we're talking about."

Henry raised his eyebrows in her direction and smiled. He crossed to Mara and pulled out a chair at the table for her. "As I was saying…" he began again, taking a seat next to her.

Furious, Malini turned her back on the conversation, which left her staring out at an empty dance floor.

"You look amazing, Malini," Jacob said from behind her right shoulder. "Breathtaking actually. No one here can hold a candle."

She turned toward him. "What about Mara?"

"What about her? I said no one." Jacob's face was gravely serious. "I just wanted you to know." He backed away toward the table and took a seat next to Mara, who was deep in conversation with Henry.

Malini watched him go, a warm melty feeling creeping through her chest. She sat down next to Henry, which at the round table left her facing Jacob. For a moment, there was no one else in the room. Their eyes met across the bursting silver centerpiece, and it was all there in his face, a mutual agreement that they'd come with the wrong people. There was still something between them.

"Ranch, Italian, or French?" A waitress leaned over Malini's shoulder with a tray full of salad dressing options.

"French," Malini said. Henry was quick to mimic her response although he didn't seem to recognize any of the flavors. The waitress ladled the dressing onto the salad that had magically appeared in front of them. When had that happened? Maybe at the same time as Dane had taken his seat next to her.

"So what do you guys think?" Dane waved his hand at the decorations.

"It's perfect!" Jacob said, a little too quickly. Malini nodded enthusiastically.

Dane beamed. "I thought you would like it!" He wore a white tux with a lavender cummerbund, an odd choice considering he didn't have a date. A pair of white wings were strapped to his shoulders. "Too bad Gideon isn't here, right?"

Malini laughed. Gideon would stand out like a beacon anywhere he went in his angel form. The comment reminded her how much she missed him. Gideon had been such a great help to her, the only help she'd received before her initiation. She hoped watching over Katrina wasn't too much of a burden for him.

Although she went through the motions of forking it in, chewing, and swallowing, she barely tasted her food. It felt like a string or a very strong magnet was implanted in her chest, and every five minutes or so she would find her attention drifting back toward Jacob. It didn't help that Henry and Mara were deep in conversation, which left her ample opportunity. Thank goodness for Dane. He was chattering on about how they found a company to donate the wings and halos.

"Would you like to dance?" Jacob asked. When had he made his way around the table? Malini glanced at the dance floor, filling fast as couples finished dinner. She was going to say that she should have the first dance with Henry, to be polite, but out of the corner of her eye, she saw him rise and take Mara's hand. They scurried toward the dance floor as if they were afraid she might say something if given the chance. She gave up on propriety and reached for Jacob's hand.

"I'd love to." She rose from her chair and allowed him to lead her to the floor. The music was slow and he pulled her into his chest. She ached to close that wretched inch between them, to grab his face and dig her fingers into his hair. She reminded herself that he was here with someone else. He'd kissed Mara. The act itself was bad enough but when she considered the timing it was so much worse. She could've died during the initiation and he was passing the time making out with someone else.

"Don't do that. Don't leave me again," he whispered into her ear.

"What do you mean? I'm right here."

"Your body is, but your mind is somewhere else. You're thinking about it, about what I did."

"How can I not think about it?" Her eyes stung but she refused to cry.

"I told you before, I didn't initiate it. I should've done more to stop it and sooner. I admit that and I'm sorry. But do you want to go on like this? Staring at each other across the table like we're twelve?"

She rolled her eyes and put some space between them as they swayed to the music.

"Don't deny it. I saw the way you looked at me. You know as well as I do that we're supposed to be together."

"I told you, Jacob. We're not destined for each other like I thought. We don't have to be together. If you want Mara, you can have her."

"I don't want Mara."

"Then why did you bring her?"

"For the same reason you brought Henry."

"I like Henry."

"You also like cheese, and by the chemistry or lack of it between you two, I'm guessing Henry is a close second."

She was about to protest and say with certainty that she liked Henry better than cheese when a scream rose up from the center of the crowd. Malini pivoted toward the sound, the smell of Watcher scorching her nose.

"Jacob, they're here!" she yelled.

The crowd parted. People ran for the exits. Malini saw him then, the man in the light-gray suit. He could have been one of the other students' parents if it weren't for two things: he had an obsidian blade held against the neck of Amy Barger, and he reeked of Watcher.

"Come here, Healer, or the girl dies." The man's voice hissed like fire doused with water.

"Who are you?" Malini asked, remaining exactly where she was.

"You Soulkeepers never recognize me as you should. You'd do well to remember my face. I can do things for you that He never would." His hair was blonde and meticulously groomed, and like all Watchers he was tall and muscular, as attractive as a movie star. Watchers could change their appearance at will, which meant they chose to be forever beautiful. But Malini knew what lingered beneath the false exterior.

"You're a Watcher. Are you some kind of leader?"

He jerked back in offense, pressing the blade into the girl's neck. Amy screamed and a drop of blood trailed down her throat.

"I am the morning star! I am the leader of all!" he seethed.

Malini recognized the biblical reference. "Lucifer!" she said. Jacob and Mara came up behind her, flanking her right and left. Henry fell back, inching his way toward the door.

"Where do you think you're going, Death?" Lucifer asked.

Henry froze, his chin lowering. "You know I cannot choose sides."

"This time my side has chosen for you to *stay in this room*!" Lucifer seethed. All the doors to the gym slammed shut and locked themselves.

Most of the students had made it into the hall but a few stragglers pressed themselves against the metal bar handles of the gym doors. One of them was Dane. He'd had plenty of time to get away. Malini wondered briefly why he'd dallied, if it was Amy or them he was concerned about leaving.

Lucifer's eyes burned in her direction and Malini was shocked how much they reminded her of Henry's. "I invite you to join me, Malini. A second flood is coming and this time I own the ark. Join me and you shall be the new world's first queen, revered by all. I promise you this. I have seen the future and this time, I win. Come now. Join me and I will spare this girl and your friends."

The blood increased its flow down Amy's neck. The top of her white dress was soaked with it. Tears flowed down her cheeks and tiny sobs escaped her. Gathering her courage, Malini walked toward Lucifer, knowing each step could be her last. "You can't see the future, Lucifer. No one can."

"Stupid girl. You could be great. You could be powerful!" He grabbed Amy's chin and wrenched it to the side, eliciting a high-pitched squeal.

Malini shook her head and glanced back at Mara and Jacob. "No, thanks. I'm happy being me."

"Cord said you'd be self-righteous."

"There's one thing Cord didn't tell you about me, Lucifer."

"What?"

"I've gone through some changes—" Lightning quick Malini grabbed his wrist with her left hand and yanked the knife away from Amy's throat. She used her foot to shove her out of the way. Beneath her hand, Lucifer's flesh bubbled against hers.

He laughed and pulled her closer. "You're quick. But I live in Hell, sweetheart. I love the burn. You'll see. When we're home, you'll come to enjoy it, too."

She had a second to regret her decision to attack him before she was lying on the floor under a folding chair and Mara was holding her hand. Lucifer was frozen above her.

"Sorry. You're going to have a bruise tomorrow but I couldn't touch you while you were touching him or he wouldn't freeze. I used the chair to knock you out of his arms."

"Thanks," Malini said, rubbing a sore spot on her shoulder.

"That's a very powerful gift," Henry said from his spot near the door.

Mara jumped, clutching Malini's hand tighter in surprise. "Why the hell aren't you frozen?"

"Death stops for no one, Mara. My existence isn't ruled by time."

Malini rolled her eyes. "As interesting as this is, can we get the hell out of here?"

Mara pulled Malini over to Jacob, reaching for his hand. He snapped out of it, relieved to see Lucifer hadn't taken

Malini. Next stop was Dane, who woke slower than the others.

"What the f—" His mouth dropped open. Malini felt his grip loosen with his surprise and squeezed his fingers.

"Stay with us, Dane. We're getting you out of here." Malini tugged his arm until he nodded.

"Shit!" Mara said, when they reached the door. It was still locked. She kicked at the metal bar.

Jacob called water from the glasses but the mechanism was locked by magic not by mechanics. "I can't open it!"

Henry strolled to the door and with a wave of his hand flung it open. He turned back toward them in the doorway. "Like I told Lucifer, I am not allowed to take sides. But as he chose to use his power unfairly to lock me in against my will, I choose to be freed. Let me be clear, I am not helping you, Soulkeepers. Death is a neutral party in the battle between good and evil. But should you choose to follow me through the open door, I will not prevent it."

He turned and strolled down the hall. Mara launched herself through the closing door, pulling the other Soulkeepers and Dane along with her.

"What about the others?" Dane said, gesturing his head toward the crowd of students frozen in various states of running in the parking lot.

"I'm not strong enough to take more. No offense, Dane, but since you're not a Soulkeeper, it's taking a tremendous amount of energy to bring you along." Mara was already shivering, her lips taking on a blue tinge.

"No offense taken. Just glad to be here."

Jacob tugged them toward his truck. "Come on. He's after Malini. Don't worry about the others. We need to get her out of here."

"No." Malini stood her ground. "When I touched him, I saw inside his mind. The ark that he spoke of—it's full of people, not animals. The increase in missing persons … it's the Watchers, Jacob. They're taking the weak to farm later when they're living above ground. After they kill off all of us, they plan to live up here and in order to do that they need flesh. Human flesh. All of these people? Lucifer is just mad enough to take them all. We can't leave them. They're defenseless!"

"Too late," Mara whispered. "I can't hold it any longer." Malini felt Mara's icy grip drop away.

All hell broke loose in the parking lot as people returned to running and screaming. A car swerved to avoid hitting them where they stood.

Mara's knees gave out. Malini lurched forward, breaking her fall with her arms. Jacob and Dane came to her aid, catching Mara before her head hit the concrete.

"I'm really drained, guys. I've got to sit down," Mara said. Her words came out slurred.

They carried her to Jacob's truck and propped her up in the passenger seat. Without warning, an explosion flattened them against the rusted blue exterior. Lucifer sauntered from the flames and twisted metal that were once the doors to Paris High School and pointed at Malini. "I tried to be reasonable. I tried to work with you, but you're not worthy of me." He held up his hands toward the night sky. "Take them! Take them all!"

Black smoke erupted in a great circle around the parking lot. When the smoke cleared, Watchers surrounded them. Malini turned, panic seizing her by the throat. People screamed, diving into the closest vehicle and locking the doors behind them. If only a simple door lock would be enough. There were twelve Watchers in all and they hadn't even bothered to disguise themselves. They stretched their bat-like wings and surveyed the chaos with yellow snake eyes.

A rush of water flew past her into Jacob's palm. He circled his arm, the broadsword forming in his hand as he rushed the nearest one. Malini turned frightened eyes toward Mara. Behind the windshield, her pale body slumped in the seat, her eyes focused downward toward her lap. Could she heal her? Malini looked at her left hand, flexed the fingers. There wasn't enough time.

Dane had made it to his truck but instead of locking himself in, he pulled a length of chain from the back. As the Watcher to her left attacked Malini, Dane leapt forward and swung that chain into the side of its reptilian head.

As scared as she was, she couldn't run and leave Dane, who wasn't even a Soulkeeper, bravely fighting her battle. Black blood oozed down the Watcher's temple. The creature snatched up the end of the chain and yanked Dane forward into its talons. He screamed and that's when Malini moved in.

Left hand extended, she closed the space between them, landing her healing palm over the creature's face. The burning was instantaneous but she held it firm, willing the thing dead. It hissed and clawed at her wrist. It was enough for Dane to get free. Blood dripped from the back of her arm where the talons dug in. It was her blood that saved her. A drip fell on the creature's chest and the Watcher dissolved into a rancid fog.

She turned back toward Dane. He'd taken on another Watcher. Jacob was fighting three more. And, to her relief, Gideon, Dr. Silva, and Lillian had arrived and were holding off the other seven. But they were tiring, and her wrist had already healed itself. Besides, she could only bleed on one at a time and her healing hand was scorched. She needed help and she knew just where to get it.

Digging her fingers into her elbow, she peeled back the glove from her right hand. She extended her skeletal hand in front of her, reaching out with that new part of herself that felt each corpse buried beneath the earth. There was a cemetery less than a mile from the school. She could feel it.

Her power hooked in and she retracted her fingers, pleading, beckoning the dead to come to her aid. They responded, their plodding pace drawing nearer as she pulled-pulled with her bone fingers.

Jacob's sword sliced the neck of a Watcher to her right, but she did not lose focus. Sweat dripped down her face and her gut cramped as the heat of her power flamed within her. Still she pulled. And then they arrived.

The dead of Paris were in various states of decay. Some were skeletons, held together by her magic and nothing more. Some looked freshly dead except for a dangling eyeball or an ear dripping maggots. But it was the ones in the middle that were terrifying. Half decomposed, they dragged their decaying flesh toward the Watchers, pawing, clawing at the black flesh. The Watchers were stronger, tossing the zombies aside easily, but the dead were many and they kept coming.

Malini fell to her knees in the parking lot, the red dress ripping against the pavement. She was soaked in sweat, panting with the effort. And she was burning alive. Blisters bubbled up from her right arm, across her chest and neck and down her left.

She watched a dead man sink its teeth into a scaly black neck. Jacob took advantage of the distraction. One-two-three heads rolled past her. Dr. Silva landed a ball of fiery energy in another and it dissolved in the purple magic. Gideon plowed a fist into yet another. The effect was the same as her blood, the Watcher evaporated. The parking lot filled with the smell of rotting, burning flesh.

Burning flesh … her flesh. Malini collapsed to the concrete and watched her zombies succeed in pulling apart two more Watchers. And just as she was about to lose consciousness, she heard Lillian's war cry, and watched her knife sail into the last Watcher's head.

The last thing she heard before she released the dead was Jacob's scream. "*Nooooo!*"

Then everything went dark.

Chapter 29
Sacrifice

Mara's arms were useless weights in her lap. At least she'd succeeded in texting Dr. Silva for help. She'd seen them arrive: Dr. Silva in a pillar of smoke, Gideon in a ray of light, and Lillian with her staff.

Crap! What was Malini doing? The bones of her right hand bent at the fingers. Was she gesturing for Mara to come? She couldn't. She was too weak.

Mara sank deeper into the seat when she saw them come. The zombies were something out of a nightmare. Decaying flesh fell from the bones as they plodded toward the Watchers. Holy shit, that hand of Malini's could raise the dead!

Sweat cascaded down Malini's skin. She'd raised an army. Over thirty zombies had descended on the parking lot. But the battle was taking time, time that bubbled in second- and third-degree burns across Malini's flesh. She couldn't keep this up for long.

Lillian slid her knife into the last Watcher's head and Mara thought that it was over. But then two things happened at once: Lucifer, who had disappeared after calling in the Watchers, reappeared, grabbed Dane, and dematerialized in a puff of black smoke, and Malini, who had fallen to the concrete moments before, stopped breathing.

"*Nooooo!*" Jacob yelled.

The zombies retreated back to their graves as Malini lay limp. The skin of her arms, shoulders, and torso was black and peeling, her hair wet from her own sweat. But she was dead. Mara knew it as much as she knew her own heart was still beating. Her body was too still.

Jacob fell on his knees next to her, feeling for her pulse. "She doesn't have one," Mara said to the windshield.

He started CPR. Two breaths, thirty chest compressions, two breaths, thirty chest compressions. The other Soulkeepers had formed a half-circle around them, hands folded helplessly as they wondered if the last Healer was dead. And Mara knew she was.

From the west, Henry appeared, pupils red with burning flames. He walked hesitantly toward Malini, and Mara knew what he would do. He was there to take her soul, to move her on to Heaven or Hell. That is what Death did. Mara looked at her bell. Death stopped for no one. Her Soulkeeper power couldn't delay the inevitable.

Jacob breathed into Malini again. He needed more time. Until Death took her soul there was still a chance they could revive her.

Mara opened the car door, sliding out of the passenger's seat and onto shaky legs. She had to do something. And the only other power Mara ever had to wield had nothing to do with being a Soulkeeper.

With what little energy she could muster, she ran to Henry, thrusting herself in front of that fiery gaze and throwing her arms around his neck. She ignored his look of surprise and planted her lips on his, pressing her body against him. She ran her nails through the back of his hair, licked her tongue across the crack of his lips, and pressed her hips against his.

Henry responded, his arms circling her waist. And when he did, she could feel the death creep into her. The coldness seeped into her lips first, then down her torso, her legs, her toes. She was dying. But what a way to die! She'd never felt this passion, this want for anyone. In the back of her mind she knew that what she had done was suicide, but it was more important that Malini live. There were other Horsemen, but only one Healer.

The icy death filled her and then she was falling, slipping away into black nothingness in the arms of Death himself.

＊ ＊ ＊ ＊ ＊

Jacob was running out of air. Part of the problem was he'd started crying, which distracted him from the CPR. He couldn't lose her. He knew the world needed Malini; she was the last Healer. But he needed her more. He was her other half and no matter what she said about him having a choice, it didn't seem so. If he lost her, he'd lose himself. He knew that now.

He was faintly aware of Mara running past him. Counting, he pressed his hands into Malini's chest and tried to ignore the way the burnt skin shifted under the pressure. One of his tears fell from his face and landed on her chest. He didn't care if anyone saw him cry. This was the absolute worst thing that could ever happen.

Where the tear fell, the blackened skin faded to gray. Another tear dropped and then another. The spot turned pink. Jacob stared at that pink spot. More tears fell: more pink spots. Of course! Water healed her!

With everything he had he called it from the ground, scooping her into his arms as springs gushed from cracks in the pavement and washed over him. He rocked her gently. The water flowed, washing away the black, and then the gray, and then the pink, until they were soaked to the bone and Malini was whole again. And then, as the water receded to its place in the ground, she gasped.

Jacob had never heard a more beautiful sound than the air rushing into her lungs. He pulled her into his chest. He should've been embarrassed that he was weeping like a baby, but for some reason it didn't seem to matter at all. Pulling back, he ran his hand over her dripping hair and met her wide, golden stare.

"Are they gone?" she stammered.

"Yes," Jacob said, "You did it. You killed them all."

She licked her lips, seeming to notice for the first time that she was wet and in Jacob's arms.

"Malini, you said that I wasn't your purpose. You're wrong. I know we have a choice. I don't think a person's destiny is forced on them. But you are my destiny, Malini, because I choose you. And not just because we can heal each other or because of some symbol on a strip of paper. I choose you because every part of me knows that it's right that we're together. It's not how it *has* to be, but it's how it's supposed to be."

She raised her left hand and placed it on his cheek. "And so it will be," she said. "Because I choose you, too."

His lips met hers. For some reason, at that moment, Jacob had a vision of a dark-haired woman in front of a loom. She was tying a knot in the cloth she was weaving. By the way the thread was wrapped and pulled, he knew this knot could never be undone.

Epilogue

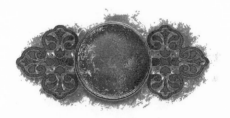

When the Paris Daily newspaper came out after prom, the headline read **School Bombed: One Missing**. An unidentified man had held a student hostage and bombed the school before fleeing. The students, who were hysterical and dressed like angels and demons, had varying, although equally confusing, stories about what had happened. Police blamed their fuzzy memories on the stress of the event.

In a gothic Victorian home on Rural Route One, five Soulkeepers sat around a coffee table knowing the truth. The real reason for the memory gaps was Dr. Silva's tea, administered to each student before they were allowed to leave. Dane Michaels wasn't simply missing; he was taken.

And a girl named Mara, who none of the students had ever heard of, had given her life to give the world a chance.

"We never found her body," Lillian said hopefully.

Gideon shook his head. "Mara is dead, Lillian; Death took her. You don't come back from Death's hand."

"What about Dane? Do you think Lucifer took him to Nod? Should we go after him?" Jacob asked.

"I doubt it. Lucifer knows Dane is special to you. He wants to use him as bait. It's you he wants, Malini," Gideon said.

Malini flexed her right hand within her flesh glove. She looked at them with resolve. "I know what needs to be done," she said. The entire morning she'd sifted through miles of fabric on the other side. The woven choices running through her fingers, the past and present, laid out for her to see. Panctu spoke the truth. She could see the future, or several possible futures, in their strands.

She stood, rubbing her hands together in front of her chest. It wasn't logical that she should be their leader. She had the least experience of anyone. But she'd been born for this. "We need to reopen the school in Eden. Lucifer will be back and he will be stronger than ever. He'll find a way to translate the list. We need to find the other Soulkeepers for their protection and for ours. The school will be a safe place to get organized until we know what we're up against."

"I can't go there," Dr. Silva said sadly. "Neither can Gideon. Eden is for humans only."

"I need you here," Malini said. "Working to find out more about what Lucifer is planning and how we can rescue Dane. Lillian will lead the revival of the school."

"Me?" Lillian asked. "I'm not a teacher!"

"You will be," Malini said, hoping to sound reassuring.

"Jacob and I, we'll find the others. We'll bring them to Eden to train and when Lucifer strikes, so will we." She brought her right fist down on the table so hard she could feel the vibration through the floor.

Gideon looked at the side of Dr. Silva's head scornfully. The distance between them was noticeable and Malini got the sense that he hadn't quite spoken his piece about her conjuring the list. They had a long way to go to find their way back to each other.

She reached behind her neck and unlatched her necklace. Leaning forward, she placed the red stone on the table between Gideon and Dr. Silva. "You need this more than I do," she said.

"Why?" Gideon asked.

"You'll know when the time is right."

Gideon looked at the stone and frowned.

Malini held her hand out to Jacob. "Come. There's nothing more we can do today. Let's go home."

She wasn't sure which home she was talking about, but it didn't matter. If he was with her, she was home.

* * * * *

In a place between places, Death jogged up the stone steps of his castle, hands full with his contraband. Through the door and down the hallway he strode, knowing that he kept a terrible secret. He'd broken the rules. It was only a matter of time before someone found out. And then, who knew? He had tampered with the very fabric of their world. But what punishment did you dole on Death?

Up the stairs and into the third room on the right, he paused inside the doorway. Her beauty blew him away. Stretched out across the blood-red sheets, she was a sleeping goddess, a latent power. He set the coffee and pastries on the bedside table and sat down on the edge of the bed. Stroking the hair back from her face, he leaned in to kiss her, knowing that the act was harmless now. She was already dead, although fully in her body. Undead might be the better word for it.

Their lips met and hers responded, her hand finding the back of his head, her mouth working on his as if she might consume him. Hungry. Wanting. He pulled back first.

"I brought you breakfast," Henry said.

Mara opened her eyes. "Later, Henry," she said.

She rolled her hands in his shirt and pulled him to her.

Other Books in The Soulkeepers Series

Return to Eden (Book 3)

Dr. Abigail Silva has waited over 10,000 years for redemption and a chance at a real relationship with the angel she loves. But when you're made from evil itself, it's hard to remember if salvation is worth the wait. With Lucifer's plan coming to fruition, she must decide if God's offer of humanity is all it's cracked up to be, or if a deal with the devil is the more promising solution.

Soul Catcher (Book 4)

Dane Michaels has been to Hell and back and isn't interested in repeating the experience. But as a human caught up in the Soulkeeper's world, his life isn't exactly his own. No one can explain why Dane was allowed through the gates of Eden, but it's changed everything. Now, the only one who can make him feel safe is Ethan, the telekinetic Soulkeeper with a dark past and a heart of gold.

When Malini asks Dane to be part of a mission to find the last Soulkeeper, Cheveyo, more than one team member thinks she's tempting Fate. But Malini suspects Fate has had a hand in Dane's life for some time and that he could be the key to unraveling Lucifer's latest plan of attack.

Lost Eden (Book 5)
Rules. Balance. Consequences. War.

When Fate gave Dane the water from Eden to drink, she did more than save his life. She changed his destiny. Since the beginning, a covenant between God and Lucifer has maintained a tenuous peace, balancing Soulkeepers and Watchers and the natural order of things. Dane upset that balance the day he became a Soulkeeper. Fate broke the rules.

Now, Lucifer is demanding a consequence, requiring Fate to pay the ultimate price for her involvement. God intervenes on the immortal's behalf but in order to save her soul must dissolve the covenant and with it the rules, order, and balance that have kept the peace. A challenge is issued. A contest for human souls begins. And the stakes? Earth. Winner take all.

The Soulkeepers are at the center of a war between Heaven and Hell, and this time nobody, anywhere, is safe from Lucifer's reach.

The Last Soulkeeper (Book 6)
The end is near.

Just when the Soulkeepers think they've established a foothold in the war between Heaven and Hell, the playing field shifts. Enraged by Cord's disappearance, Lucifer replaces his right-hand man with the Wicked Brethren, three Watchers so formidable even their own kind fears them.

The Soulkeepers struggle to survive in an increasingly deadly world while continuing to defend human souls. How far will they go when saving the world means sacrificing their most precious team member?

Other Books By G. P. Ching

Grounded

A seventeen-year-old girl discovers she's the product of a government experiment, when her father's illness causes her to leave her isolated community.

Return to Eden (Excerpt)
Book 3 in The Soulkeepers Series

Chapter 1
Forbidden Fruit

Abigail Silva knew she was dreaming, the kind of bittersweet dream that could float away on the current of a waking breath. Clue one was the June snow. It drifted down around her as she walked into her garden, the delicate plants unbothered by the winter storm. The lush foliage harkened back to the days when Oswald's soul still warmed the air.

Gideon waited for her, closer than usual, close enough to cause her skin to prickle from the heat in real life. A lock of wild auburn hair cut across his forehead and his pearl-white wings folded against his back.

Holding her breath, she reached for him. Slow. Tentative. Would her imagination allow her this one sweet experience? Or, would her touch fill them both with scorching pain as it did in the waking world?

Soft ecstasy. There was no pain, no burn. Her shaky exhale ruffled the feathers where her hand made contact. Gentle but eager, she stroked his wing downward, moving her caress to his upper arm. The light from within him shimmered between her fingers. Touching Gideon was touching heaven. She inhaled the smell of sandalwood, orange blossoms, warmth, and light.

A smile spread lazily across Gideon's face, reaching all the way to his emerald-green eyes. He raised one rugged palm. She pressed her cheek into his hand. Those pearly wings enveloped her body, protecting her from the snow, a thoughtful but unnecessary gesture considering her Watcher skin couldn't feel the cold.

Abigail decided as long as she was dreaming, she'd make the most of it. For centuries she'd wondered what it would feel like to kiss Gideon. His lips were full, parted, waiting. Tilting her chin, she pressed her mouth to his. She closed her eyes, desperate to cling to every detail of the honey-sweet kiss. How long could she remain here in this fantasy? She vowed to fight waking with everything she had.

Pain. Abigail opened her eyes. Gideon was gone, replaced with the cold, blond illusion that the devil preferred to use. She might have screamed but there was something in her mouth. What had tasted like honey now moved bitter and rough on her tongue. She gagged, pitching forward. A cockroach crawled from her bottom lip and dropped to the dirt.

"Lucifer!" she spat.

"You remember me, Abigail? So glad I made an impression the last time we were together. Have ten thousand years of absence made the heart grow fonder?"

She scrambled away from him. "Am I still dreaming or is this real?"

"Both, my dear. You are still asleep, and this is very much real."

Pulse racing, she tried to turn for the gate but her legs refused to obey. When Lucifer wanted an audience he got one. "Why are you here? I thought we agreed to go our separate ways after the fall?"

"Separate ways, yes. But I hadn't counted on you going the opposite way. You've crawled straight back to God. The list of Soulkeepers I stole from you—I believe you had no intention of sharing it with me. You're helping Him now. Unfair, Abigail. You were supposed to be mine."

"We had an agreement."

"I've never had a problem breaking an agreement." Lucifer rolled his eyes and spread his hands.

"What do you want, Lucifer?"

"I want you, Abigail. I need your help with something, help only you can give me. Join me and we will conquer this Earth, and I will make you a queen over it."

"Not interested," she said, crossing her arms over her chest. "I know how your promises work. Sure, you'll make me a queen—Queen of the Damned. Queen of the Broken. The most sorrowful of the sorrowful. No thanks. You forget I have free will. I choose not to help you."

Lucifer stepped closer, smoothing his blond hair with his hand. "Oh, but I can give you something God can't. I can give you Gideon."

As dangerous as it was, she leaned toward his face, her teeth coming together in an audible snap. "You've been breathing too many sulfur fumes. Gideon is not yours to give. God has promised us humanity. Gideon and I *will* be together."

"When? Pity about God's promises. He's always sketchy on the details. You never thought it would take this long, did you? For all you know, it could be another thousand years." Lucifer picked at something under his nail, then held his hand to the light, admiring his manicure.

"God always keeps His promises," she said softly.

"Yes, eventually. Like Moses reaching the promised land." Lucifer turned his attention back toward her and pressed his finger into his bottom lip. "Oh wait, that didn't work out so well for him, did it? What did He promise you, exactly? Did He say He'd make you human when evil is vanquished from the Earth? Clearly that's never going to happen. Must be easy for Him to make promises He never has to keep. And they call *me* the Lord of Lies."

"I'm not talking to you about this. I'm not helping you." She shook her head and backed away.

"If I ran things, Abigail, Gideon could fall. I could make him like us. If you were both Watchers, you could touch. You could kiss. And you could be together, forever. Human bodies age and die. What I offer you is permanent."

"Gideon would never fall. He's too good. He's not like me and he's definitely not like you."

"You underestimate your influence over him. He'd fall for you. You know he'd do it for you. He's already left heaven for you. It's not that much farther to go."

Abigail squared her shoulders and did a very stupid thing. She met Lucifer's eyes directly. There was a reason the name Lucifer meant morning star. With his bright blond hair, golden skin, and aqua blue eyes, he was attractive by human standards. But the way he glowed was like looking into the sun. Everything about him pulled her under, a deceivingly bright undercurrent that promised safety but delivered death. Only, somehow, Lucifer made her thoughts twist until she believed she wanted to die. She was desperate to die.

She tried to remember what she planned to say to him. Even when she looked away, she couldn't shake his hold on her. He smelled just like Gideon. He gave off light like Gideon. She buried her face in her hands and began to weep.

"There, there, Abigail. I know my presence is overwhelming. Take some time. Think about my offer. I'll be around." Where his hand touched her shoulder, Abigail's skin squirmed like it was covered in maggots. "I'm *always* around."

In the time it took her to lower her hands, he was gone. The darkness swallowed her, suffocating her under ten thousand pounds of weight, as if she were buried alive in her own subconscious. She struggled against the pressure, flailing her arms and kicking into the blackness. With a scream, she awoke tangled in her sheets. Black snakeskin fingers gripped her pillow. Her fingers. She'd lost her human illusion.

With a few deep breaths, she extended her hand and focused her energy. The scales transformed into smooth alabaster skin. A perfect French manicure took the place of her talons.

"Another nightmare?" Gideon asked, approaching from the corner of the room where he slept standing up. His light spilled over her.

"Yes."

"I don't suppose you're going to tell me about it."

"Don't be like that, Gideon." Abigail swept her platinum hair behind her shoulders. The blade-straight coif, her preferred illusion, cascaded elegantly down her back. She hugged her knees to her chest.

Gideon climbed onto the bed, kneeling beside her carefully. "Abigail, you've been secretive and obviously tortured since Lucifer stole the list of Soulkeepers. These nightmares, they mean something. You're feeling guilty. You should talk about it."

As well meaning as the sentiment was, Abigail felt the edge of his words. It was as much an accusation as a suggestion. "I've told you, Gideon. I don't feel guilty about what happened. I conjured the list of Soulkeepers for a good reason. Who knows how many lives I saved by calling Mara here to help slay those Watchers in Chicago? We needed help and I got it. There's no way I could have foreseen Lucifer would get the list."

Two fists came down on the bed in front of her, so hard it bounced her backward on the mattress. "No, Abigail. The Healer told you to wait. You should have waited. Don't you get it? You acted in your own will. You invited this mess."

"No, *you* don't get it, Gideon. We have free will for a reason. We're supposed to think for ourselves, to do what we know is right even when it means breaking the rules. And let's not forget that I was smart enough to place a spell on the list to keep Lucifer out. He can't read the list because of me."

"He wouldn't have the list at all, if it wasn't for you."

Abigail crawled forward, until she was so close to Gideon her face burned. "I don't feel guilty for what I've done. But let's be honest, you feel ashamed. Right now you are wondering whether your choice to join me on Earth was worth it. You are wondering if I am worth it."

Gideon lowered his eyes.

"That's all the confirmation I needed." Abigail bounded off the bed.

Gideon reached for her, the muscles in his shoulder bunching with the effort. "I know you are worth it, Abigail. You've always been worth it. But I wonder if we will ever be in the same place at the same time. I can't understand what you did because I don't think like you." He narrowed his eyes and his reaching hand formed a fist. "We are together, every day, but still worlds apart. Lately, it feels like galaxies apart."

Abigail folded her arms over her chest and turned toward the stained-glass window. "Maybe we are."

"I do not regret coming to Earth for you, but this is hell. Having you but not having you is *hell*. No, I don't understand how you stay as strong as you do, or how you have the courage to risk our future on what you *feel* is the right thing to do." He crawled off the bed and took a step toward her. "I don't have that kind of courage."

With a deep sigh, Abigail pivoted to face him. "I'm not ready to give up."

Gideon shook his head. "I won't give up. Ever."

Silence wedged itself between them, but it wasn't because there was nothing left to say. The words that waited in the corners had sharp edges. Words like that could do permanent damage if flung too hard at the one you loved.

"Do you want to watch the sunrise from the tower?" Gideon asked.

"Can you still hear it?"

"No, not really. Sometimes, when it breaks the horizon, I think, maybe. There's a smell like citrus and seawater. But it only lasts a second and then it's gone. I'm beginning to think it's more memory than reality."

"I can't even remember it anymore. All I can see is the light."

Gideon's face twisted and he looked away from her.

"It's still worth seeing." She spread her arms. "It's worth seeing with you."

He ran toward her and leaped, transforming into the red cat before landing in her embrace. She scratched him behind the ears and sank her lips into his plush red fur. "Don't worry, my love. I can fix this. If we keep believing, if we keep moving forward…"

Gideon purred.

"Trust me. Trust me and I promise I'll do whatever it takes to keep us together."

About the Author

G.P. Ching is the bestselling author of The Soulkeepers Series, and Grounded. She specializes in cross-genre YA novels with paranormal elements and surprising twists. As of March 2014, over 300,000 copies of The Soulkeepers Series novels have been sold since the series debuted in 2011. The Soulkeepers was named a 2013 iBookstore Breakout Book.

G.P. lives in central Illinois with her husband, two children, and a Brittany spaniel named Riptide Jack. Learn more about G.P. at http://www.gpching.com and more about The Soulkeepers Series at http://www.thesoulkeepersseries.com.

Sign up for her exclusive newsletter at http://eepurl.com/hvAAk and be the first to know about new releases.

Twitter: @gpching
Facebook: G.P. Ching
Facebook: The Soulkeepers Series

Reviews are gold to authors! If you've enjoyed this title, please consider rating or reviewing it at your place of purchase.

Acknowledgements

Special thanks to the following people for their help with Weaving Destiny.

Karly Kirkpatrick, Michelle Sussman, and Angela Carlie, you are more than co-workers, you are friends. Friends that feel like family. I'm serious when I say that knowing you has been a rocket launcher on this series.

To friends Michelle Moore, Michael Brennan, and Robin Brennan, thank you for reading Weaving Destiny when it was still a baby manuscript and helping it to grow with your wonderful suggestions.

Thank you to Dawn Malone who always brings a bit of cleverness to the manuscripts she critiques. I owe you big for helping me to see Weaving Destiny in a different light.

Thanks to Adam Bedore of Anjin Designs for the amazing cover art. I think it's the best out there.

To my amazing readers, thank you for your endless enthusiasm! And thank you to the book bloggers and reviewers who gave The Soulkeepers a chance.

Finally, thanks to the #fridayflash community, along with the other authors I've come to know on twitter and facebook, who have been so supportive of The Soulkeepers.

Book Club Discussion Questions

1. At the beginning of the book, Malini thinks Jacob is her destiny. Do you think there is only one person in the world who you are destined to fall in love with?

2. Malini has to face deadly challenges throughout Weaving Destiny. What do you feel is the source of her strength?

3. Do you think that parents who are immigrants to the United States like Malini's have unique challenges with raising their children and adapting to American culture?

4. Mara comes on strong to Jacob. What would make a person try to woo someone they knew was in a relationship? Do you think her background had anything to do with it?

5. Malini grows up and discovers who she is in Weaving Destiny. Do you think it's possible for someone to love another person fully before they know and love themselves fully?

6. The Healer cannot die without Malini's help. Jacob says it is not murder but mercy. How do you feel about this

scene? In your opinion, are there any circumstances in the real world (people or animals) when killing would be mercy?

7. Mara and Death have an instant connection. Do you believe in love at first sight?

8. Malini views snippets from her past to learn ways to approach the problems of her future. How do you feel your past experiences have prepared you for your future? Are any experiences truly a waste of time?

9. Dane and Malini have a special friendship in Weaving Destiny. Do you think the relationship was completely platonic or did one of the parties secretly want more?

10. Mara has a formidable skill in Weaving Destiny, the ability to stop time. If you could stop time, what would you do with that power?

Made in the USA
San Bernardino, CA
11 September 2014